"What is it, Molly? A headache? I'll carry you to bed."

Pietro reached out to her but she stopped him. "No need. I'm okay, truly. It's just that I remembered something."

To her surprise, instead of invoking a smile, her news made his dark, straight brows draw together. "You did? Something important?"

"Anything's important, surely?" A smile tugged her mouth wide. "I remembered gardening!"

"Gardening?" Pietro looked confused.

"Silly, isn't it? You'd think I'd remember the big things first, like you. Or coming to Italy."

"You don't remember any of that?" His voice sounded strained, making Molly abruptly aware that Pietro had also been through an enormously tough time.

If she knew him better, she'd have reached out and covered his hand with hers. A tremor passed through her, a surge of longing. She wanted so badly to connect with him, to smash through the invisible barrier between them. But she didn't have the nerve.

He was still a stranger, after all.

Growing up near the beach, **Annie West** spent lots of time observing tall, burnished lifeguards—early research! Now she spends her days fantasizing about gorgeous men and their love lives. Annie has been a reader all her life. She also loves travel, long walks, good company and great food. You can contact her at annie@annie-west.com or via PO Box 1041, Warners Bay, NSW 2282, Australia.

Books by Annie West

Harlequin Presents

Seducing His Enemy's Daughter
Inherited for the Royal Bed

One Night With Consequences

Contracted for the Petrakis Heir
A Vow to Secure His Legacy

Secret Heirs of Billionaires

The Desert King's Secret Heir

The Princess Seductions

His Majesty's Temporary Bride
The Greek's Forbidden Princess

Wedlocked!

The Desert King's Captive Bride

Visit the Author Profile page
at Harlequin.com for more titles.

Annie West

—————

HER FORGOTTEN
LOVER'S HEIR

H HARLEQUIN PRESENTS®

Recycling programs
for this product may
not exist in your area.

ISBN-13: 978-1-335-41985-9

Her Forgotten Lover's Heir

First North American publication 2018

Copyright © 2018 by Annie West

This edition published by arrangement with Harlequin Books S.A.

For questions and comments about the quality of this book, please contact us at CustomerService@Harlequin.com.

Printed in U.S.A.

HER FORGOTTEN
LOVER'S HEIR

This story is for all those readers who tingle with anticipation at the thought of an amnesia story. Thank you for your enthusiasm for my earlier book: *Forgotten Mistress, Secret Love-Child*. Your feedback is what prompted this new story. I hope you enjoy it!

CHAPTER ONE

SHE WOKE TO a sense of disorientation.

Blinking, she took in the dimly lit room. The visitor's chair, bedside table and small window. Now she knew where she was. Rome. The hospital they'd brought her to after she'd been knocked down on the street.

Yet, instead of feeling calmer, her pulse quickened. The sense of disorientation didn't ease. How could it when everything beyond this room was a blank?

Her name.

Her nationality.

What she was doing in Rome.

She didn't recall anything.

Impulsively, she reached out to the bedside table, fingers running over the small comb and vanilla lip-balm that were the only possessions she could call her own. Her clothes had been so torn and bloodied they were unwearable and whatever bag or wallet she'd carried was missing.

She shut her eyes, forcing her breathing to slow. Forcing down the fear at not knowing anything.

After all, she did know some things.

She wasn't Italian. She spoke English, with only a smattering of tourist Italian.

She was in her twenties. Pale-skinned with regular, if ordinary, features. She had grey-blue eyes and tawny hair that looked limp after the blood had been washed out.

And she was pregnant.

Her breath hissed in as she struggled with fear at the thought of being pregnant, nameless and alone.

The amnesia would pass. The doctors were hopeful. Well, *most* of them were hopeful. She was determined to cling to that. The alternative was too horrible to contemplate. She'd feel better in daylight when the medical staff bustled around the ward. Even the continual barrage of tests would be a welcome change from lying here, utterly alone and...

Something tugged at her senses. The hairs on her nape rose and her skin tickled with the awareness someone was watching her.

Slowly, since quick movement made her head ache, she turned towards the door.

She blinked, then blinked again. Wasn't it enough that her memory was shot? Had she begun hallucinating too?

In the shadowed doorway stood a man who surely didn't belong here. Tall, broad-shouldered and lean enough to wear his dark suit to elegant perfection, he looked like a model for designer menswear. That square jaw, the hint of a groove low in each cheek and those soaring cheekbones were all ultra-masculine and stunningly attractive.

A fillip of emotion stirred in her belly. Surprise, obviously. And attraction. As a distraction from self-pity he was perfect—the epitome of the 'tall, dark and handsome' cliché.

Except, as he stepped into the room, she discovered he wasn't anything so simple as a pretty face.

There was an underlying toughness about him that made her skin prickle. He was the sort of guy who made designer stubble sexy instead of effete. His nose was strong rather than suave and his eyes hinted at shrewd, calculating intelligence. His height made him dominate the room and the effect was magnified when he stopped by her bed.

She tilted her head up, heart pounding.

'Who are you?' It seemed vital she sound calm, though everything inside her quickened.

Maybe he was some fancy consultant. That might explain his lack of bedside manner. No cheery smile, no platitudes about time being a great healer. No stethoscope. She couldn't picture anything so mundane draped over that superbly fitted suit.

His eyes bored into hers and she saw now why they looked so unusual. They were brown flecked with gold and glowed with an inner fire, their colour unexpected given his olive skin and dark hair.

His silent scrutiny made her uncomfortable. 'I said—'

'You don't remember me?' His voice was honey and whisky, velvet and steel, and it would have made her hang on his every word even if he'd recited from a phone book. But when he implied...

She scrambled to sit up then winced as the movement made her head pound.

'Are you all right? Should I call someone?'

Not a doctor, then.

'Should I remember you? Have we met?'

Something she couldn't identify flared in those golden eyes.

'Do you know me?' She leaned towards him, silently pleading for him to say he did.

Someone somewhere held the key to her identity.

'I—'

There was a bustle in the doorway and one of the doctors entered. The chubby one with the kind eyes who'd reassured her when the fear she'd never regain her memory had grown close to terror. He burst into excited Italian, questioning the man at the bedside. The stranger responded, those grooves in his cheeks more pronounced, as if carved by concern. Back and forth they talked, the doctor voluble, the stranger answering with terse responses.

As if she weren't there!

'Can one of you *please* explain who this man is and why he's here?'

Instantly the doctor turned towards her. Which was when she registered that the tall stranger hadn't once taken his eyes off her. Even as he'd spoken with the medico his scrutiny of her had been constant.

She shivered, pulling the light cotton blanket higher up her body.

There was something about the intensity of his regard that made her feel naked. Not simply naked beneath the flimsy hospital gown, but as if he could strip her character back to the private self she kept hidden from the world.

Which was completely fanciful, as she had no idea what sort of person she was! If he could read her innermost character... Good—maybe he could enlighten her!

'My apologies.' It was the doctor who spoke. 'We should have spoken in English.' Then he smiled, his eyes bright with enthusiasm. 'But we have excellent news for you.'

She swung her gaze back to the man standing silent at her side. Her tongue swiped her suddenly dry lips. 'You know me?' Despite her best efforts the words were shaky.

Abruptly he nodded. 'I do. Your name is Molly. You're Australian.'

Molly. An Australian.

She sank back, barely aware of the doctor leaning in to prop up some pillows behind her.

Australia. That explained why she spoke English, not Italian.

Molly? She frowned. She didn't feel like a Molly. Did she?

Her frown became a scowl as she tried and failed to feel any familiarity with the name.

She swallowed, petrified as she realised even her own name was foreign to her. She'd assumed that, once she had more information about herself, her memories would kick into gear. But the revelation of her name hadn't worked any magic at all. There was still nothing but that dreadful foggy nothingness.

'It probably sounds strange, hearing it for the first time again, but you'll get used to it.'

She stared up at the tall stranger, registering his reassuring tone. How had he known about her panic when she didn't recognise her own name?

'Are you a doctor too?'

He shook his head and she heard the doctor murmur something under his breath.

'Yet you know me?'

Gravely he nodded. Why didn't he look happy or at least relieved to help her discover her identity?

'And?' She gritted her teeth. Did she have to plead for every nugget of information?

'You came to Italy working as an au pair for an Italian-Australian couple.'

'An au pair?' She tested the idea on her tongue. Yet, once again, there was no spark of familiarity.

'A nanny. A child minder.'

She nodded impatiently. She knew what an au pair was. Yet, how did she know, when even her own name was totally unfamiliar?

Molly. Was that really her name?

'You're sure you know me? You're not confusing me with someone else?'

Was that sympathy in his eyes? Whatever his expression, it was swiftly masked.

'Absolutely sure. You're a teacher but gave it up for the chance to come to Italy.'

'A teacher...'

'You love children.' Something in his voice, something sharp and hard, snagged her attention. Was it imagination or was the golden light in his eyes more pronounced than before?

Yet for the first time she accepted his words without question. Yes, she *did* love kids. She could visualise herself as a teacher. Not that she could remember any individual children, but for the first time in this odd conversation his words struck a resonance deep within her.

She'd been dumbstruck to discover herself pregnant in such extraordinary circumstances. Terrified at the idea of bringing a child into the world, not knowing who she was or who the father was. Yet even her fear couldn't completely obliterate her wonder at the new life she carried. Maybe, once her memory returned, she'd actually be excited about it.

She sank back against the pillows and offered a tentative smile.

Instantly he reacted. His nostrils flared, as if he drew in extra oxygen, and his eyes…

She didn't have time to worry about his eyes, no matter how gorgeous they were. This was about her. Molly… Molly what?

'What's my last name?' Once she had that she could find her past, locate her family and friends and begin to knit her life together again. Her fingers tightened, clenching the thin blanket. *If* she could get her memory back. If she wasn't doomed to lose her past for ever.

The idea sent a shaft of fear right through her.

The tall man's gaze flickered towards the doctor, who nodded.

'Agosti. Your name is Molly Agosti.'

She frowned. 'Agosti?' Once more she waited for her subconscious to recognise the unfamiliar name. Nothing. Not even the faintest quiver of recognition. 'Are you positive? That sounds Italian. But I'm Australian.' And her colouring wasn't typical of someone descended from Italians.

'Absolutely sure.'

She'd have to take his word until she had proof to the contrary. 'And you are…?'

Did he stiffen? No, he didn't look at all put out. Yet something had changed. Surely the vibration in the air between them grew charged?

She blinked. Vibrations? Charged air? Was she a person who thought in terms of auras and unseen forces? Or was she just preternaturally attuned to this man?

'I am Pietro Agosti.'

She stared up past the disturbingly powerful hands resting on the rail at the edge of her bed and that long, elegant body.

'Agosti. But that's the same name.'

He inclined his head. 'It is.' Then the corners of his mouth curled up in a smile that made the breath stop in her lungs, even though the smile didn't quite reach his eyes. That golden-brown stare remained watchful, assessing.

Deep in her subconscious, an alarm bell sounded.

'That's because I'm your husband.'

CHAPTER TWO

HER PULSE SLAMMED past fast to frantic as she gawped up at the imposing man before her. One part of her mind atrophied in shock, another part raced in circles trying to make sense of his words.

Her *husband*? This unnerving man?

It wasn't possible.

Even forgetting for a moment his air of cool assurance and those honed, handsome features, everything about him screamed money and power. His suit must have been made for him, it fitted so perfectly. His shirt was snowy, nothing as average as mere white, and his subtly gleaming silk tie was the sort that came in a designer box. At his wrists were discreet yet intricately crafted gold cufflinks.

His hands... Her heart gave a sharp thump as she concentrated on his hands. They were large and strong but well-shaped. Seductive hands, the sort that would know their way around a woman's body. Hands adept at giving a woman pleasure.

She had a thing for sexy hands?

Of all the things she needed to know about herself, that had to be low down on the list. Except, staring at Pietro Agosti's hands, such knowledge suddenly seemed of paramount importance.

Heat flared in her cheeks and she kept her gaze fixed there rather than meet his stare, worried what he might read in her eyes. It seemed…wrong to feel that squiggle of strong reaction deep in her feminine core just looking at this man. Despite his words, he was a total stranger to her.

The hands in question were well-cared-for and there was a heavy gold signet on one finger that looked old and expensive.

He came from money, lots of it. She'd guess, based on his ingrained air of command and that ancient ring, he'd probably been born to it.

But *she* wasn't. She didn't know how she knew, but in that moment she was convinced of it.

Her face, when she'd scrutinised it in the bathroom mirror, had been ordinary. Not beautiful or intriguing. Her hair was lank and a shade somewhere between caramel and dirty blonde that surely was too ordinary to have come out of a bottle? Her hands weren't scarred or rough, but nor were they manicured. And her only jewellery was a pair of tiny gold stud earrings.

She and Pietro Agosti didn't match. How could they be married?

If it were true, then it must be *his* child she carried. The idea sent a tumble of unsettling emotion through her.

'Signora Agosti.'

Her head jerked up at the sound of the doctor's voice. She opened her mouth to reject the title he'd given her.

That wasn't her name, was it? And as for being married...

She shot a sideways glance at the tall man standing beside her bed, utterly unmoving. There was something about his stillness that unnerved her. He was waiting for something.

For her to acknowledge him?

Or for her to declare she couldn't possibly be his wife?

She frowned, the tightness in her head turning into a thump of pain in time with her quickened pulse.

When she winced the doctor bustled forward, murmuring in Italian beneath his breath as he checked her pulse and got her to lie back.

Yet all the time she was aware of Pietro Agosti looming silently beside her, tall, dark and dauntingly handsome. If the doctors hadn't assured her she'd recover fully physically, she might have wondered in her confused way if he was the Angel of Death come to take her.

She lifted her head and caught him staring. He didn't look away and she sank into the surprising warmth of his bright gaze.

Heat flared anew, this time not in her cheeks but deep, deep inside. In those female organs where her tiny embryo of a baby was lodged.

Was this the father?

Emotion sliced through her. Excitement or fear?

She settled for disbelief.

'You're *sure* I'm married to this man?' It didn't seem likely. Surely he spent his time with gilded socialites, not au pairs?

The doctor's eyes rounded and he darted an apologetic look at the taller man.

Was Pietro Agosti so important that no one ever questioned him?

A shiver snaked through her. For some reason she hadn't a hope of identifying, she baulked at the idea of being at his mercy.

His mercy? Surely that wasn't how a wife thought of her husband?

'Signora Agosti.' The doctor's reassuring tone broke across her thoughts. 'There was no doubt about the identification. Your husband was able to describe you in perfect detail before he arrived, right down to your appendix scar.'

Which only meant he was intimately acquainted with her body.

A sizzle of sensation prickled her skin. Was it a remnant of memory? The legacy of intimacy with this man? Or anticipation at the idea of him stroking those big hands across her bare skin sometime in the future?

She sneaked another look up at the sombre man beside her. As if on cue his sculpted lips turned up into a smile that would have been soothing, if it hadn't been for the shadow that looked like calculation in his eyes.

Her throat was gritty as she swallowed. Her eyelids flickered down as she fought off the headache beginning to beat in time with her pulse. It was all too much to take in.

'Let me assure you that your husband is most respectable and esteemed—'

'I think that's enough for now.' The deep voice with that sexy, husky edge interrupted the doctor's encomiums. 'Molly's obviously too tired for this tonight. It's all been a shock. Maybe we should leave her to rest.'

He was going?

Her eyes snapped open as fear hurtled through her.

What if he left and didn't come back?

What if he left her alone again, like an unclaimed piece of luggage?

What if, tomorrow, this proved to be a dream? If there was no one who knew who she really was?

Reason told her that wouldn't happen. He'd identified her and the hospital staff would know how to reach this man who was so well-regarded and respectable.

Yet the well of fear that had threatened to suck her down for days swirled anew. She couldn't face the idea of being abandoned here again.

'No! Please, don't go!'

There was a flash of something in those uncanny eyes but this time it looked like sympathy.

'Perhaps, doctor, you might give us some time alone together? I know there's paperwork to complete. I'll see you after Molly and I have spoken.'

'Of course. Yes, an excellent idea.' The doctor clearly didn't mind being dismissed. Which told her he was either glad to hand her over to someone else or that Pietro Agosti was a VIP with considerable influence. The medico nodded to Molly, assured her all would be well and left the room.

Now, alone with the man who said he was her husband, her relief dissipated. But instead of towering over her any longer he reached for a visitor's chair and sat by the bed.

'That's better. Now you don't have to crane to look up at me.'

His mouth crinkled up at one corner in the smallest of smiles but this time, for reasons she didn't understand, she felt a tug of response. Her lips twitched and her taut muscles eased a little. It was only now that she realised her shoulders had crept up towards her ears and her hands had curled into taut fists. She looked down and smoothed her hands across the bedspread.

She looked so damnably pale. Fragile in a way he hadn't expected, even when he'd heard about her injuries. He'd come immediately, riding a wave of shock and relief at the news that she'd been found.

Something inside Pietro stretched tight and hard, tension twanging like a plucked string. His chest squeezed as he read the pain etched in Molly's tired eyes.

One of the things that had attracted him to her was her warm, sunny disposition. Her ready smile and the way her eyes danced. Seeing her so frightened made him want to break something. Preferably the motorbike rider who'd knocked her over. Who, it seemed likely, had targeted her for her bag with its wallet and passport.

His staff was liaising with the police. If the person responsible was located, he'd pay dearly for his actions.

Pietro's jaw tightened at the idea of Molly lying unconscious on the road. Of her waking to the horror of not even knowing her own name.

The doctor had said her memory loss might partly

be due to shock. From the fall? Or from what had happened before she'd come to Rome?

Icy fingers of guilt gripped his throat.

Pietro swallowed hard. The accident or assault wasn't his fault. As for what had happened before…

'I'm glad you found me.' Solemn eyes held his. 'It's…worrying, not knowing who you are.'

She looked so lost, yet so determined to be brave, downplaying the fear she must feel. A wave of protectiveness washed through him.

Pietro froze. He'd thought himself immune to feminine vulnerability. He'd been inoculated against it by brutal experience. But the circumstances here were different.

He reached out to grasp Molly's hand and reassure her then stopped himself. Better to keep his distance. She looked so frail, her eyes huge in her pale face, watching him warily.

She noticed the movement but said nothing, though her brow knitted, as if she had catalogued the abortive gesture for future consideration.

It was a reminder that he needed to be careful how he proceeded. He couldn't afford to make another mistake.

'I can't begin to imagine how it feels not to recall anything,' he admitted. He half-expected her to confess it wasn't true, that she remembered something, even just the reason she'd left on the spur of the moment for Rome. 'But you don't need to worry. I'll take good care of you.'

'You will?'

He couldn't work out if she looked pleased about

that or petrified. Did he *scare* her? He knew his size could be daunting…

'Of course. You can count on me. Everything will be all right, Molly. Just give it time. You don't need to worry about a thing. I'm trying to contact your sister in Australia, to bring her over to see you.'

The tightness around the corners of her generous mouth eased and a little colour returned to her wan face, making her look more like the woman he knew.

'I have a sister?' She sounded so excited, so wistful.

'Her name is Jillian.'

'And my parents?'

Pietro shook his head, wishing he could give her better news. 'I'm sorry, Molly. There's just the two of you.'

Her face fell and Pietro felt his chest squeeze. He remembered loss only too well. Molly's pain reinforced his determination to do everything he could for her.

'But I'm very lucky to have both a husband and a sister.' Her gaze dropped from his, as if she were fascinated by the movement of her hand plucking at the bedclothes. 'I wondered if anyone would ever come along and identify me.'

There was a wealth of repressed fear behind her words and Pietro felt a surge of relief that he'd mobilised a search for her. If he hadn't, if he'd ignored that belated voice of logic telling him he'd made an appalling mistake, how long would she have been stuck here alone in frightening limbo?

The knowledge strengthened his determination. He'd acted impulsively tonight but he didn't regret it, or any complications that might arise from it. Molly needed him.

'You'll feel better when you're out of here.'

'Out of here? You mean out of the hospital?'

He nodded. 'Of course.'

'Really?' Her tentative smile reached her eyes, making them shine more blue than grey. 'They'll let me go?'

Again Pietro felt that strange sensation in his chest as he looked into her hopeful eyes. He told himself it was only satisfaction that this would be so straightforward.

'You're not a prisoner, Molly.'

'I know that. I know they've been doing their best for me.' She looked up into that brown-gold gaze and told herself there was nothing to be frightened of now. Her husband was here. The person she presumably trusted above all others.

Yet still that nervous tingle of energy ran from her nape to her fingertips and down her spine as her gaze collided with his. Each time it felt like a shock, an assault on her senses.

There was definitely a sizzle of awareness as she took in his proud features and the strength of his rangy, powerful form. Yet shouldn't there be something more? A sense of relief and comfort; of…homecoming…when she looked at him?

It wasn't relief she felt, at least not solely. There was something else mixed in there too. Something her subconscious tried to tell her, except she wasn't very good right now at reading subliminal messages.

Who was she kidding? She wasn't much good at

anything. Complex thought made her head spin and any attempt at delving into the past made the grey walls around her close in.

Defeated, she shut her eyes as her struggle to remember failed and pain rose once again.

'Molly? What is it?' His tone was sharp. Even with her eyes closed she clearly caught his sense of urgency.

Which was natural for a man seeing his wife in these circumstances. It was absurd for her to think there was something not right here.

The only thing not right is you. Your brain isn't working properly. You don't even recognise your own name! Did you really think one sight of the man you love would bring your memory flooding back?

Logic told her she'd expected too much. Yet she couldn't shake the feeling something was wrong.

The chair scraped across the floor and she opened her eyes to see Pietro Agosti striding towards the door.

'Don't go!' Was that desperate voice hers? She shot forward to sit straight up in the narrow bed, ignoring the way the movement slammed the ache in her skull from dull to throbbing.

So much for masking her fear. Faced with the prospect of being alone again, the strength she'd relied on to see her through this nightmare evaporated. '*Please* stay.'

'I was just getting the doctor. You're in pain.' Yet he stopped on the threshold, his dark eyebrows tilting down in a frown.

'Please don't leave.'

Was she always this needy? She hoped not.

How did she explain to this sexy, forbidding

stranger that she'd give anything for a little ordinary human comfort instead of more medication?

Pietro Agosti's gaze dropped from her face. She followed the direction of his stare and saw her hand was raised, stretched towards him. Her fingers trembled. She hadn't been aware she'd reached for him.

She let her hand fall and swallowed hard. Her desperation for his presence, his touch, disturbed her. Maybe because it proved she'd finally reached the end of her tether. She couldn't face being alone with her fears any longer.

'Aren't you going to take me home?' She gave up worrying about how weak that made her sound. She needed to know.

'Of course.' His voice came from right above her. She hadn't heard him cross the room. Still, she didn't lift her face to look at him. She felt as if that searing golden gaze could see right inside her, that she was *vulnerable* to this man in ways she didn't understand. While he, with his air of control and unreadable expression, was a closed book to her. Surely lovers, husbands and wives, were more…equal?

But then, what did she know? Everything was new to her. She didn't know whether to trust her instincts and the ideas that popped into her head or whether they were the product of trauma and medication.

'I'll take you home as soon as the doctor says you're free to go.'

Home.

Relief was a splintering wall, letting hope flood her. Soon. Soon she'd be away from here and her memory would come back in familiar surroundings. Surely it would?

The chair scraped again softly. Then a long arm in a dark sleeve stretched across the bed. Old gold gleamed against a pristine cuff then hard fingers closed around hers. His touch was gentle and reassuring, enfolding her hand in warmth and comfort.

He didn't say any more and she didn't look at his face, too scared of the terrible strangeness she felt when she looked at the man who was her husband.

Instead she focused on his hand holding hers, the rhythmic stroke of his thumb across her flesh. The tiny caress counteracted the sickening lurch of anxiety in her belly.

Heat spread from his touch. Tiny ripples of delicious sensation that radiated through her whole body till soon she floated, limp and relaxed, in a sea of wellbeing.

Her fingers tightened around his and he gently returned the pressure. A sigh rose in her throat even as her heavy lids flickered.

She'd been wrong.

There *was* a connection between them after all. She could feel it now. Not just the warmth and delicious sense of peace, but something else. Something vital right at the heart of her. As if a missing part of a puzzle had slotted into place and everything was all right again.

Because Pietro Agosti was with her.

Her mouth curved up in a tiny smile and her weighted lids closed.

Everything was going to be all right.

Pietro studied the sleeping woman who still clutched his hand. He catalogued everything about her, from her slender fingers and delicate wrist to her bare arm, which the Italian sun had turned a soft gold. Her rounded breasts rose and fell beneath the blanket with each even breath.

Her collarbone looked fragile, as if she'd lost weight in the last week. At the thought, regret sliced through his midsection. His hand tightened on hers till he realised what he was doing and released her. She needed sleep.

His gaze rose to her face. She was still too pale, making that smattering of freckles stand out. Her eyebrows were finely shaped and darker than her hair. Likewise, her long lashes were brown, not blonde. Her nose was even, though undistinguished, and her chin neat. The only remarkable feature was her mouth. Wide and exquisitely sculpted into a cupid's bow, it was the sort of mouth a man could fantasise about.

Just thinking of her lips on him sent Pietro's blood surging low, awakening a heavy tension in his groin.

He lifted his arm off the bed and shoved his hands in his pockets.

It was a relief he'd been able to comfort her. She'd clearly been frightened and trying hard not to show it, but his touch had helped.

He told himself he was doing the right thing. Of course he was. He'd had to act quickly and there'd been no other option. If he'd thought ahead, he'd have anticipated the complication that had forced his hand. But he hadn't been thinking clearly for days.

Pietro Agosti prided himself on his ethics, his honour. Some accused him of ruthlessness, primarily those he'd bested in a business deal or, very occasionally, an ex-lover who hadn't believed him when he'd declared he was only interested in a short-term affair.

He was honest, sometimes brutally so.

Which meant that what he did now, what he was about to do, cut across his personal code of behaviour.

Cut across! His mouth lifted in a cynical smile. Why not call a spade a spade? He was blatantly lying.

But it had to be this way, at least for now.

Pietro stifled the carping voice of his conscience. He refused to feel guilty about doing the right thing for all concerned.

It wasn't as if he was going to harm her. On the contrary, his aim was to care for her, look after her, during a time when, surely anyone would agree, she most needed his help.

He did what he did because there was no alternative.

CHAPTER THREE

THE LIMOUSINE WAS sleek and almost silent as it glided away from the hospital and onto the city streets.

Molly avoided looking at Pietro sitting beside her. Doubt about their relationship filled her. She told herself it would cease with time and familiarity. Yet it was unnerving. She didn't feel up to breaking the silence, especially after the wearing bustle of departing from the hospital. It was scary how weak she felt. How isolated from everyone.

She peered ahead of her, hoping for a sight of something, anything that might jog a memory.

There was nothing. Her heart sank as the car made its way through a city that was unfamiliar to her.

It's too soon. They all said not to expect anything yet.

But she couldn't push aside the unpalatable cocktail of excitement, fear and impatience. She'd hoped that once she got out of the hospital room, that had become both prison and refuge, memories would crowd back.

The sun shone and it was a warm day, judging by the clothes of the people on the street. In the air-conditioned car it felt cool. Or maybe that was because of the stilted atmosphere here behind the privacy screen that separated the driver from his passengers.

There'd been no ecstatic reunion with her husband. Nothing but a guarded kindness. Such as when he'd come to her bed last night and held her hand till she'd fallen asleep.

There hadn't even been a kiss!

What sort of marriage did they have?

She wasn't scared of Pietro. She'd never have gone with him if that were the case. But still he made her feel edgy.

Molly told herself he was simply a man who didn't show his feelings in public, and there'd been staff fussing about them all morning. Even the head of the hospital had made an appearance, shaking Signor Agosti's hand and all but bowing them out of the building.

Besides, Molly was injured. It was natural Pietro would treat her carefully rather than sweep her into his arms and kiss her senseless.

Her cheeks fired at the idea. How would it feel, being scooped up against that hard, lean body?

She'd dreamed of him in the night, of his hand holding hers as she lay in her narrow hospital bed. In her dream that hard, gentle hand had touched her elsewhere, exploring thoroughly, driving her wild with an urgent, carnal hunger. Molly had woken, damp between the legs and hot all over, in an empty room.

Was that memory or imagination? Pietro knew her body well enough to describe her appendix scar. Maybe what she'd considered an erotic dream was a memory. Perhaps it was part of her brain's reawakening.

'How are you doing?' Pietro's deep voice set off a shuddery response inside Molly, as if she was still in the grip of that erotic dream. 'Is the temperature okay for you?'

Her blush intensified because he'd noticed it.

That was another thing: Pietro watched her continually. Molly told herself it was good that he was concerned for her comfort and so solicitous.

'It's just right. Thanks.' Deliberately she made herself turn to the man beside her on the back seat.

In broad daylight he was just as dauntingly, devastatingly good-looking. Like one of the beautiful people you saw splashed on the pages of magazines and TV shows about the rich and famous.

Not that she'd describe him as beautiful. That arrogant nose and no-nonsense jaw were powerful rather than pretty, and his expression of reserve and cool consideration proclaimed he was nobody's fool.

Yet Pietro had sat holding her hand last night till she'd fallen asleep. He'd been uncomplaining this morning as they'd waited for the results of yet more tests. Then he'd sat through a long consultation with every doctor on the premises, it seemed, plus senior administrators. Molly was convinced so many staff had appeared because Pietro Agosti had been there.

He was a VIP yet she knew nothing about him. He'd kept the conversation focused on her, her chances of recovery, symptoms and care. There'd been no chance for private conversation. There had been too many people around.

'How did you find me?' She fixed on those golden-brown eyes looking back at her.

'My people were searching for you.'

'Your people?'

'My staff.'

'You have staff?' As soon as the words spilled out, she felt foolish. Of course he had staff. This was a private limousine and Pietro knew the driver's first name. Plus there must be someone keeping his clothes in such pristine order. Molly couldn't picture him pressing his shirt and shining his own shoes to that mirror gloss before stepping out of the door.

He shrugged. 'I run a company. I assigned some trusted staff to help.' Not a small company, then.

'You didn't just look for me yourself?' She'd pictured her partner scouring the city for her.

Pietro's expression turned grim. 'You *disappeared*. It wasn't a one-man job. I employed an investigation firm too.' His voice grew even more clipped and Molly realised with a burst of relief that must be how Pietro dealt with emotion, by keeping it tightly leashed.

Maybe she'd been influenced by that popular image of Italians as extroverted about their feelings. Clearly Pietro wasn't. He did that whole controlled, macho thing to perfection. But it warmed her heart to know he'd been worried about her.

'How did I disappear?'

'Sorry?' His eyes narrowed, as if taken by surprise.

'How come you didn't know where I was?' Pietro stared back silently. 'I take it I didn't just pop out for a carton of milk?'

'You went to Rome and—'

'*Went* to Rome? You mean we don't live here?' She was sure he'd given an address in the city to the hospital authorities. But then she still felt a bit foggy. Surely she hadn't been mistaken?

'We'd been staying at the family villa in the country. You wanted to come to Rome and I couldn't go with you because of other commitments.'

Molly sat back against the luxuriously upholstered

seat and wondered what it was about his words that
sent a shimmer of unease through her. Surely there
was nothing unusual about them living in the country? Except that, with his suave tailoring and severe
good looks, Pietro seemed utterly urban. She couldn't
visualise him in faded jeans and a T-shirt.

Though she'd love to try. She had a suspicion he'd
fill them out to perfection.

She put her unease down to their odd situation,
married yet strangers. And possibly to Pietro's un-
blinking regard when he spoke, as if checking she accepted everything he said. Why wouldn't she? Did he
think she'd forget what he told her? She might have
lost her long-term memory but she recalled everything that had happened since she'd woken in hospital,
though sometimes she found it hard to focus.

'The trouble was, once you got to Rome you vanished.' There it was again, that tightness in his deep
voice. Molly heard it and knew Pietro repressed strong
emotion. It was a male thing, she figured, not to let
others see vulnerability. Plus, he probably didn't want
to stress her with how badly her disappearance had
affected him.

'I didn't mean to.'

He looked into her face and his features softened.
'It doesn't matter now. That's all over.' After a moment
he reached out and squeezed her hand briefly. Instantly
Molly felt better. Her fingers wrapped around his and
clung, till the limousine took a tight curve and Pietro
swayed back into his own corner.

'But we have a place in Rome too? We're going
there now, aren't we?'

He nodded. 'We are. It's not far. But don't get your

hopes up. The place has just been completely redecorated, so I suspect it's not going to awaken any memories for you.'

'You really are a mind reader.' Last night, as he'd watched her, Molly had been convinced of it.

'Hardly, but it seemed logical you'd expect it to.'

Molly shrugged, trying to stifle disappointment. 'At least with my own things around me I'll feel more at home. You never know, even something as simple as my old clothes might spark some recollection.'

She thought disconsolately of the red comb and vanilla lip-balm now nestled in the smart designer handbag Pietro had produced for her this morning. So far none of her possessions had opened the door to her lost memory.

Nor had the clothes he'd brought in this morning. Expensive pewter-coloured shoes and a plain silk dress that had looked almost drab on the hanger, but which had clung elegantly and transformed her into a stylish stranger. Yet she hadn't felt at home in the outfit, despite the luxury of the gossamer-fine silk and exquisitely dainty underwear.

Her mouth curved bitterly. She didn't care about being stylish, but she hated the fact Molly Agosti was still a stranger to herself.

'Ah, I'm afraid you'll have to wait a little longer for those.'

'Sorry?'

His eyes met hers. 'For your own clothes. You brought some with you to Rome but because our place here was still under wraps, with paint fumes and the designer adding the final touches, you didn't stay there.' He paused and for a second she thought she read uncertainty in Pietro's face.

The impression swiftly passed. He spread his hands in a speaking gesture and lifted his shoulders. 'Unfortunately you forgot to give me your accommodation details before you went out and had your accident. Your luggage is still in your room in Rome. But we haven't managed to track down where that is yet.'

'You don't know where I was staying?' It seemed strange.

He nodded, his expression regretful. 'It would have been a simple matter to have my secretary arrange your accommodation, but the trip was on the spur of the moment, and you've always been…independent. You don't like a fuss.'

Molly sank back in her seat, her mind reeling. 'So these clothes aren't mine?' She plucked at the fine dress which was lovely and clearly pricey but which felt somehow not *her*. Which was an absurd idea, when she didn't know what sort of person she was.

'Bought for you by a personal shopper. A very discreet woman.'

Pietro's sharp gaze must have registered her dismay, for he leaned towards her, once more covering her hand in his.

'It's okay, Molly. It will all be okay.' His voice hit that low gravel and suede note she'd heard in her dreams last night.

A shiver passed through her, a ripple, not of dismay but of awakening. For in response to Pietro's touch her body began to come alive. Heat stirred in her belly and her breasts tightened against the lace of the brand-new bra.

She was disappointed, horribly disappointed, that at journey's end she wouldn't have anything of her very own to help her regain her memories. But with Pietro leaning close, the warmth of his body invading hers, it wasn't panic she felt. It was desire. Awareness. Attraction.

The constraint she'd felt around her impossibly gorgeous husband cracked. Their carefulness with each other was due to her unusual situation. For beneath it was a deep channel of passion. That passion ran strong and true now as they edged their way towards an understanding of new boundaries.

It said something about her husband's character that he didn't press her, expecting her to act as if everything was normal between them. He must be hurt by the fact she had no recollection of him. Yet he was patient and restrained, respecting how difficult this was for her.

Molly smiled up into the dark face so close to hers, her heart filled with thankfulness and joy.

'I'm so lucky I've got you. Thank you, Pietro.'

Pietro's lungs stalled, his breath faltering as Molly looked up at him, her generous mouth pulling wide in a smile that was all gratitude and happiness.

Her smiles had always been heady things. When she was carefree, they were like golden sunshine on an endless summer day. When she was amused, her smile beckoned conspiratorially, inviting you to share the joke. And when she was aroused her smile turned sultry and irresistible, a siren's weapon with the power to stifle even the sternest voice of caution.

At the moment it wasn't the voice of caution that

bothered him but his conscience. She'd accepted everything he'd told her easily, which of course was what he wanted. But then to have her so *grateful* to him…

Pietro thrust aside the quibble of conscience. There was no place for such niceties here.

He was doing the right thing. His goals were the same as hers—to look after her and the baby.

What could be wrong with that?

Yet he wished she wouldn't look at him that way. It wasn't just that it evoked an unnecessary pang of guilt. Her adoring look stirred other feelings too, feelings he didn't have time for. This situation was precarious enough without adding further complications.

He turned his head and looked outside satisfaction rising as he saw where they were. 'Good. Here's our place now.'

'Our place' turned out to be a lavish top-floor apartment sprawling across the footprint of a whole building.

Molly felt her eyes bulge as she took it in. It looked like something from an upmarket home-decorating magazine, each room more discreetly luxurious than the last, all in shades of white or cream. She reached out to touch the celadon figure of a horse, the sole touch of colour in a huge living room, then tugged her hand back. It was probably some priceless antique.

Her breath quickened and her pulse too as she gazed through the wide open doors to the formal dining room, large enough for a banquet. Even the sleek, minimalist study nearby screamed expense with its spare designer furniture and exquisite artwork.

Did she *really* belong here? She felt like an interloper.

Firmly Molly told herself it was because the place had been recently remodelled, with perfect taste and a restrained opulence that absolutely screamed wealth. She sensed she hadn't been born to this sort of money, even if Pietro had.

She darted a glance at the tall man beside her who'd stopped to silence the quiet buzz of an incoming call to his phone. How much she had to learn about the man she'd married! And about herself.

It was a daunting prospect but she stilled the whisper of unease sidling along her nerves and tried to project a confidence she didn't feel. *Fake it till you make it*—wasn't that what they said? Molly had a disturbing feeling it would take a long time to feel comfortable in such surroundings.

Pietro introduced her to a smiling housekeeper, Marta, explaining that she spent the days here, leaving each evening.

Molly nodded and said something suitable, surprised by how daunted she felt at the prospect of having staff to cook and clean for her. It felt…odd. As if she wasn't accustomed to employing someone to do what she could easily do herself.

Except, exploring the prestigious residence at Pietro's side, she realised it was probably a full-time job keeping the place in such pristine condition. Everything gleamed spotlessly, from the antique mirrors to the long lap pool on the roof garden. Even the lush potted plants flowered in profusion with not a single dying leaf.

If it had been left to her, half the plants out there would be sick. Her only gardening talent was to kill the plants she tried to nurture.

Molly froze mid-step, halfway across the terrace.

How did she know that? Did she know it or just imagine it? Was her mind filling in the vast gaps of her life with stories that weren't real? What about her self-consciousness at having a housekeeper? Surely she was used to having staff, since it was how she and Pietro lived?

'Molly? What is it?'

Instantly Pietro was there, his gaze concerned, his mouth tight. 'Come, sit down.' He gripped her elbow and ushered her towards a shady pergola and a stylish iron chair with a cream cushioned seat.

Ecru, Molly thought hazily as she sank onto it. Like everything else in the apartment, the outdoor furniture featured shades of white. Yet she'd bet the posh designer who'd created this showpiece wouldn't call the cushions anything as ordinary as creamy white.

A broad palm covered her forehead, as if checking for a fever, and Molly knew a momentary urge to lean into Pietro's touch, seeking comfort in his physical presence. But he dropped his hand and hunkered before her, eyes searching.

'What is it, Molly? A headache? I'll carry you to bed.'

Pietro reached out to her but she stopped him.

She shook her head, not trusting herself to speak. For her instant response to the idea of him carrying her was *yes, please*. Not because she needed to lie down but because she wanted the comfort of Pietro's arms about her, holding her close.

The one sure thing she'd discovered since meeting him was that she felt better when he touched her.

Molly craved that comfort so much she was afraid

it made her weak when she needed to be strong to get through this difficult time.

She cleared her throat. 'No need. I'm okay, truly.'

He sat back on his heels and she curled her fingers into the thick seat cushion so as not to give in to temptation and reach for him. He really was the most amazing looking man. Particularly when he stared at her with such intensity, such concern, in those stunning eyes.

'It's just that I remembered something.'

To her surprise, instead of evoking a smile her news made his dark, straight eyebrows draw together.

'You did? Something important?'

'Anything's important, surely?' She cocked her head, trying to read his still features, then gave up. A smile tugged her mouth wide. 'I remembered gardening!'

'Gardening?' Pietro looked confused.

'Silly, isn't it? You'd think I'd remember the big things first, like you. Or our wedding. Or coming to Italy.' Molly shrugged and sank further into the comfortable seat, revelling in the sun's warmth out here on the terrace after her time cooped up in hospital.

Slowly he nodded. 'You don't remember any of that?' His voice sounded strained, making her abruptly aware that Pietro had also been through an enormously tough time. Think of having someone you loved disappear without a trace. And then to have her turn up and not remember you!

No wonder he was tense. He'd been through the mill too.

If she'd known him better she'd have reached out and covered his hand with hers. Or smoothed out the faint frown on his wide forehead.

A tremor passed through her, a surge of longing. She wanted so badly to connect with Pietro, to smash through the invisible barrier between them. But she didn't have the nerve. He was still a stranger after all.

Her smile faded. 'I'm sorry. I probably raised your hopes. It's nothing really, not even a clear picture in my head. Just the knowledge that I'm a dreadful gardener. I used to joke and say I had a black thumb, not a green one, because of all the plants I'd inadvertently killed off.'

Excitement raced through her. She hadn't remembered that last bit at first. The knowledge had come to her as she'd spoken the words. It was like being on a ribbon of road unfolding before her in real time but not knowing what was coming up around the next curve.

Eagerly she concentrated on the idea of tending plants. She tried to conjure a mental picture to go with the words that had popped into her head and the certainty that this really was a memory.

But there was nothing. No matter how hard she tried.

'That's marvellous!' Pietro's belated enthusiasm almost made up for her failure to form a concrete picture of the past. 'Didn't they say your memory would start returning?' His mouth curved as he stood. It must be a trick of the light that gave his smile a cool edge, as if it didn't reach up to his eyes.

'Now, sit here and I'll get you a cool drink. I don't want you to overdo it.'

Molly shook her head. 'No need.' Tempted as she was to stay, sunning herself in the open air, she had other priorities. 'What I'd really like is a long, hot shower or maybe a bath.'

At the hospital they'd removed the last bandage and she'd had a quick shower before changing into the clothes Pietro had brought. Yet she felt as if she still smelled of institutional cleanser and the indefinable scent of hospital that had filled her nostrils too long.

'If you're sure.' He stood back so she could rise. 'But then have a rest, and later we can talk. You need to build up your strength gradually.'

Molly was about to reassure him that she was healthy and that she'd had more rest than she'd liked. But she did feel fatigued. Just from the stress of leaving hospital! The realisation dampened her excitement. How long before she was back to normal?

'Perhaps you're right.'

Besides, Pietro wanted to look after her. She shouldn't throw his concern back in his face.

His solicitousness warmed her. How foolish she'd been when he'd arrived at the hospital, thinking there was something darkly brooding and dangerous about him. He'd just been worried about her.

How much more concerned would he be if he knew she was pregnant?

She needed to tell him and soon. But not yet. According to the hospital, the pregnancy was in the very early stages. Pietro hadn't mentioned other children so this would be their first. She wanted to choose the right moment to break the news.

Besides, she needed more time to adjust to being Molly Agosti. To get to know her husband and herself. She had so many questions, so many things she needed to understand.

So she didn't blurt out the news of the baby. She had no idea how he'd react. Would he be thrilled?

Maybe they'd been trying for a while. Or would it be unexpected? No, definitely better to wait a little longer before throwing that news at her husband as well. For now they had enough to deal with.

Which was why Molly didn't demur when Pietro showed her to a gorgeous bedroom, asked again if she needed anything then left, closing the door behind him. For a moment, maybe two, she'd wondered if he'd stay with her, fold her in his arms and take her to bed, not for sex, but for a long overdue cuddle.

Of course she wasn't disappointed when he didn't. He was being careful of her boundaries, aware that to her he was a complete unknown.

Yet in her heart of hearts Molly longed for the comfort of his embrace.

She slipped out of her shoes and wriggled her toes in the plush softness of the rug at this end of the room. At the far end the bed sat on a raised plinth with a gorgeous headboard of stylised roses climbing up a metal frame.

Quickly Molly turned away. She was *not* going to think of Pietro on that broad bed. Or of herself naked and spread-eagled on the counterpane, her fingers gripping the headboard as a tall, dark-haired man settled between her thighs.

Molly choked back a gasp of excitement mingled with shock.

Was *that* a memory? Heat seared and her mouth tipped up in a grin as she thought of her returning memory beginning in the bedroom. But it wasn't to be. It was simply a case of wishful thinking.

Yet between her legs a pulse started up and her muscles softened.

Simply from imagining Pietro in bed with her.

How long had it been since they'd had sex? Had they been abstaining for some reason or did she have a naturally sensual nature?

So many questions. So few facts. After she'd showered, she'd begin finding out more. This morning it had been enough to get away from the claustrophobia of the hospital and trust Pietro to bring her home.

Soon she'd get more answers.

Sighing, she crossed the floor and opened a door. Instead of the bathroom she found herself in a dressing room. Molly stopped, eyes widening, as she took in the luxurious space. Customised storage for shoes, bags, boots and hats. A deeply padded day-bed, presumably for reclining on while deciding what to wear. Racks of clothes in a multitude of colours and styles. Her dazed eyes took in a bright sundress and a tailored suit. There were dresses that sparkled and swept low towards the floor and skirts that flared or fell in straight lines.

Slowly she pivoted, surveying the range of feminine clothes it would surely take months and months to wear. Had they, like the clothes she wore, been bought while she'd been in hospital? Was it all on loan while she decided which items she wanted? She'd have to talk with Pietro.

But as she turned she discovered something else. There was no men's clothing in the space.

Frowning, Molly backed out and returned to the bedroom.

There was another set of doors. But as she turned the handle she discovered they led out onto part of the roof terrace, made private by screens of green foliage that blocked it from the rest of the garden.

Molly turned and crossed the room, her feet silent on the cool floor. She pushed open another door and there was a bathroom, an airy space full of exquisite creamy marble flecked with gold.

Ignoring the call of the sunken tub, and the rain shower big enough for a small crowd, Molly spun round, surveying the bedroom.

No more doors, which meant no walk-in closet for Pietro.

Nor were there any signs of male habitation. There was nothing on the bedside tables, desk or even on the long sofa facing the bed.

Pietro didn't share this room with her.

Which begged the question—exactly what sort of marriage did they have?

CHAPTER FOUR

THE SUN WAS low in the sky as Pietro sat on the roof terrace, pondering his situation.

There were too many chances for failure. At any moment, if Molly's memory returned, he'd be scuppered. She'd put up so many barriers it would make what he had to do almost impossible.

Not that that would stop him. He was determined to get what he needed. Because he played for the highest stakes.

Pietro might have been born to wealth and privilege, but he'd known tragedy, deceit and disappointment. Those had galvanised him into a man who didn't play at life. He worked single-mindedly to get what he wanted then keep it.

At the age of ten his world had been ripped asunder. His beloved parents and little sister had been killed in a freak accident. He'd known then what it was to feel utterly alone and vulnerable, cut off from the world. As the years had passed and he'd learned to deal with the terrible sense of isolation, he'd vowed to build a life that contained everything he'd lost.

The success of the family business, which had been tottering towards insolvency by the time he was old enough to take control, was a result of his determination. As CEO, he thrived on challenge.

Pietro's mouth twisted. His personal life was less successful. *Less successful.* There was a laugh.

His marriage to Elizabetta had been a fiasco. He'd been so distracted by the prospect of having a family of his own, by the child she'd said she was carrying, that he'd ignored the warning signs. How had he not seen earlier that his ex-wife was a gold-digger and liar? How had he allowed himself to fall for the sham pregnancy?

Simple. She offered what you longed for. What you've dreamed of since you were a kid.

Belonging.

Family.

Somehow Elizabetta had sensed that and exploited his weakness. But he'd learned quickly. Now she was out of his life. Yet the yearning remained. For blood ties, for a family of his own.

With Molly he'd get just that. The thought sent anticipation ripping through him. Finally, he'd have it all.

A sound drew his attention and he looked up. Molly stood, paused, in the doorway. His pulse kicked and tension coiled in his belly.

Yet it wasn't the success of his careful scheme that excited him as Molly stepped out onto the terrace.

It was sex.

Heat burgeoned low in his body and his pulse thrummed as he took in her slim figure in fitted white capri pants and a sleeveless blue top, her narrow feet in low white sandals.

Pietro frowned at the stark intensity of the hunger grabbing at his insides. He wanted to march over and sweep her into his arms and straight back to bed.

He'd looked in on her a few hours ago and had stood far too long staring down at her as she slept. She'd been curled up like a child on top of the covers. But the glimpses of pale breast and thigh at the gap in her robe had been pure, seductive woman. He'd been on the verge of kissing her awake and joining her on that bed when he'd come to his senses, remembering she was still an invalid.

It had been the same the night they'd parted in Tuscany. Despite his fury and the sour taste of disgust on his tongue, he'd lusted after her then too. Neither pride nor common sense had eradicated his hunger for this woman. That, above all, explained why he'd lost his temper so monumentally.

In his eyes what she'd done had been unforgivable, but even worse was the fact that he still wanted her in spite of it.

Now that anger was gone, stripped away by the truth. Everything had changed. Except his desire for Molly. It was so strong, so electric, he wondered that she didn't pick up on it.

He smoothed the frown away and raised a hand in greeting. *'Ciao, bella.'*

She gave him a tentative smile and made her way towards him.

The late sun burnished her tawny shoulder-length hair into waves that showed highlights of gilt and amber. Possessiveness struck. Pietro remembered threading his fingers through those thick tresses, fascinated by the colour. She'd dismissed it as somewhere between brown and dirty-blonde and had spoken of dyeing it one day.

Women were strange—never happy with what they had.

'Sleep well?'

She nodded. 'Better than I remember ever sleeping.' Her mouth twisted into a rueful smile and she shrugged. 'Which isn't saying much since my memory only goes back days.'

'One day at a time, *cara*. You'll get there.'

Despite his need to take advantage of her memory loss, Pietro didn't like to think the amnesia might be permanent. He'd spent a long time interrogating the medical staff about that. The one thing they'd all agreed was that no one knew for sure, but most were hopeful her memory would return given time.

Meanwhile he was determined to look after her, keep her safe.

And ensure the success of his own plans.

'Thanks, Pietro.' She hesitated over his name as if shy, and instantly he was hurtled back to the day they'd met. She'd been self-conscious yet charming. He'd been intrigued as he'd watched her stiffness disappear as soon as she'd interacted with her young charges and forgotten him.

Now she stopped by the table, her head angled as if to scrutinise him better. Instantly he was alert, conscious of the need to be careful.

'Is something amusing? You're smiling.'

'Am I?' Pietro was surprised. He might have been amused at the memory, but he hadn't actually smiled. He'd been told more than once that he kept his emotions well-hidden. It was a useful trait during business

negotiations and over the years it had become instinctive, as he preferred to keep his feelings private.

She took the chair opposite and sank down. 'Not
exactly smiling, but one corner of your mouth twitched
and your eyes looked different.'

Pietro stared, astounded that she'd sensed his mood
from such slight evidence. No one else read him so
easily.

He needed to be even more careful than he'd anticipated. Had Molly always been able to sense his
thoughts and feelings? The idea disturbed him. Pietro
was used to being the one in control, the one reading
others, not being an open book himself.

Marta appeared with a tray.

'*Grazie.*' Molly smiled at the older woman and accepted a soft drink.

'*Prego, signora.*' Marta served Pietro's glass of
wine and a platter of *antipasto misto*.

Pietro nodded his thanks then turned back to Molly.
'You haven't forgotten your Italian, then?'

Just how much *did* she remember? He hadn't probed
earlier for she'd looked so fragile. Yet he had to know,
for it would determine his next move. Was it possible
she recalled more than she admitted?

She shrugged. 'Much good it will do me. I can say
"please" and "thank you". I know some food and the
days of the week, but I get the numbers confused.' Her
eyes fixed on him, grey now rather than blue. 'Was I
ever fluent in Italian? I don't remember. Not a thing.'

The sunny smile she'd given the housekeeper faded
and her eyes grew shadowed. She blinked, her mouth
pursing, as if to stop it trembling. Molly wasn't dis-
sembling. She really knew nothing of her past. He was

so caught up in his own deception he was too ready to expect it in others.

Molly's distress tugged at something deep within. He reached for her hand resting on the table and covered it with his. He ignored the heat that flared when they touched.

'Give it time.' He made his tone upbeat. 'But I'm afraid as far as Italian goes you weren't ever proficient. You'd just started learning.'

'There was I hoping that when my memory came back I'd find myself fluent.' She smiled just a little too widely and he read the fear in her eyes despite her light tone. Something struck his chest and his hand tightened. He wanted to help but there nothing he *could* do. The experts had told him that. Yet such impotence made him uncomfortable. He was used to decisive action.

'I can fill in some of the blanks for you.' Even though he'd much rather *not* talk about the past he wasn't accustomed to lying and, though he had no doubt he was pursuing the right course of action, he'd prefer to avoid more untruths.

Molly's smile rewarded him. Gone were the clouds in her eyes, replaced with sunny pleasure.

'Fantastic! I have so many questions. But first, what amused you when I came out? Was it to do with me?' Her hand slid from his and began twisting a tiny pearl button on her pale blue top. Her other hand lifted to her hair then fell to her lap.

She was nervous. About how she looked?

Surely not? Molly was slim and sexy in a fresh, wholesome way, quite different from the sophisticates he usually met in Rome.

'I was remembering the day we met.'

'Really? Tell me!'

It was as if he'd ignited a spark inside her. She sat forward eagerly, her pink lips parting in a soft smile and her eyes turning a hazy blue. He could always tell when Molly was happy or excited because her eyes looked more blue than grey.

'It was at my villa in Tuscany.'

'You have a villa in Tuscany too?' Then before he could answer she shook her head, making her hair swirl around her cheeks in a bright curtain. 'No, of course you do. It makes sense when you have all this.' Her gesture encompassed the penthouse apartment. 'I suppose you have a luxury sports car as well as the limo.'

He shrugged. 'I use the limo in the city as I'm usually busy with business calls. In the country, I prefer to drive myself.'

Which was better than saying he had several sports cars and, for that matter, a couple of other properties, including the whole of this building. For he remembered how Molly's eyes had widened in shock, first at the limousine then at the sight of his city apartment. How tentative she'd been, walking through the expensively furnished rooms, as if scared to touch anything. He didn't want her feeling even more uncomfortable. Time enough for her to learn the scale of his wealth later.

She sipped her drink then sat back, expression expectant. 'So, you were at your villa in Tuscany. How long ago? When did we meet?'

'The spring just gone.'

He watched her eyes become round. She sat forward. 'Really? Such a short time ago?' Colour high-lighted her cheeks. 'So, we're newlyweds?'

Pietro nodded and spoke quickly, not wanting to get side tracked into detail. 'We haven't been together long.'

Molly's brows knitted and she stared at her glass, her flush intensifying. 'Yet we don't share a room.'

Pietro's heart gave a mighty thud. Why had he believed for a moment that Molly would simply accept things without question?

'You need plenty of rest. The doctors were insistent.'

Plus, despite the rush of desire when he was near her, he had qualms about bedding her now. He was already taking advantage of her amnesia. If she knew all that he knew, she wouldn't be sitting here, blushing and smiling at him.

'So, I was at the Tuscan villa.' Pietro paused to make sure his diversion worked. Sure enough, Molly nodded, eager for more. 'I was working in my study.' No surprise there. He spent a lot of time working, even when he was supposed to be relaxing, or in this case recuperating from a bad bout of flu—brought on, his doctor had said, from too many hours working and not enough enjoying life. 'But this particular morning I had trouble concentrating.'

At her curious glance, he went on. 'The villa isn't alone on the property. Down the drive, on the other side of a small hill, is an old farmhouse. My cousin Chiara is a budding entrepreneur and persuaded me to let her do it up and rent it out as guest accommodation.' The agreement was she'd keep any profits too and Pietro had been happy to support her small but growing enterprise.

'I rented it?'

He shook his head. 'Not quite. A family from Australia rented it. The husband's ancestors were from Tuscany and they wanted to explore the area for several months. You came with them to look after their three young children. They just returned to Australia last week.'

Slowly she nodded, twisting her glass round and round on the table. 'That's right, you said I was an au pair.'

'Temporarily. You're a qualified teacher, specialising in early childhood. As one of the boys has learning difficulties, the parents were eager to get someone with your qualifications.'

Molly frowned. 'I gave up a teaching job for temporary work as an au pair?' Apparently she hadn't really registered that when he'd told her yesterday but she'd had a lot to take in.

Pietro leaned back in his chair, fascinated by this insight into Molly's thought processes. With her ready smile and easy going nature, when they'd first met he'd merely thought her ripe and ready for a temporary amorous adventure. It was only later he'd discovered Molly was far more complex and circumspect. Surprising, given what had happened between them. But here it was again, proof that she wasn't as carefree as she had sometimes seemed.

'You didn't yet have a permanent teaching job. I believe you'd had several temporary positions. This was a chance to travel then return to look for something long-term.'

Slowly she nodded and it struck him how hard it must be, learning about herself from someone else. It made him want to remove her anxiety as much as he could.

'You're wonderful with the children. Even when they're tired and difficult.'

Her smile made her glow, and it sent heat shafting straight to his groin. He imagined that smile in other circumstances. With Molly naked, her arms stretched out towards him.

'And that day in your study?'

Reluctantly Pietro dragged his thoughts back to the present.

'There was a problem with the pool at the rental farmhouse and it couldn't be used. My cousin begged me to let the children use mine, under strict supervision, a couple of hours a day.'

'Let me guess—I was the supervisor?'

'You were. Every day, often twice a day, you'd visit with the kids.'

'I bet you just loved having children squealing and playing when you were trying to work.'

Pietro shook his head. 'It was distracting but I didn't really mind.' For he liked children too. Wanted some of his own. It was why he'd finally begun to think again of finding a suitable wife after the disaster of Elizabetta.

Family was something money and success couldn't buy.

Pietro knew he was lucky. He had an aunt, uncle and cousins. But he longed for more. They'd never come close to replacing the close-knit family he'd lost.

He was determined to have that again.

'Pietro? Are you going to finish telling this story?' Molly regarded him quizzically.

'Of course.' He returned her stare with a smile and watched in satisfaction as she blinked and sucked in a deep breath that made her breasts rise sharply. Yes, *this* was what he wanted. No, *needed*. Molly responding to him, trusting him.

'Well, there I was, wrestling with a particularly boring report, when I heard laughter.'

She nodded. 'Most kids get noisy in a swimming pool.'

'It wasn't the children I heard. It was a woman, and her laughter was like liquid sunshine pouring through the courtyard and in through the open door. I got up and followed the sound and found three little kids and you.'

Molly's brow knitted in confusion. 'Liquid sunshine?' She sounded almost uncomfortable. As if she wasn't used to getting compliments. 'That's a very poetic exaggeration.'

Pietro sat back, surveying her, watching a betraying hint of pink wash her throat and cheeks. 'It's no exaggeration. And the best part of it was you had no idea how alluring it was. It wasn't contrived to attract attention.'

He'd learned to tell the difference. Arch looks and tinkling, musical laughs designed to snare a male made his blood run cold. His tongue soured. He'd had his fill of that.

Pietro remembered his first sight of Molly standing in the shallow end of the pool with an over-sized white T-shirt stuck to her body, revealing the outline of a dark bikini beneath. One side of her head was wet where the children had splashed her and the other was all soft, gleaming waves. And that smile...

Pietro had looked at her and felt something visceral. A claw of hunger. A throb of want. A desire to capture the brilliance of her laughter and the warmth of her kindness as she played with the kids. A need to possess that svelte, delectable body.

That, he realised, hadn't changed. He wanted Molly now just as much as he had then. It was a craving in the blood.

He had to ignore that, for it threatened to distract him, and he needed all his wits about him.

Molly stared at the chiselled features of the man before her. He exuded charisma, an aura of power and masculinity that was anything but average. Even with her impaired memory she understood that.

Pietro Agosti was the sort of man who'd make any woman sit up and take notice. His smile alone made her knees feel like jelly. And when he stared at her that way...

She'd looked in the mirror. She'd seen the ordinary woman looking back at her. She wasn't some fatally attractive seductress.

'Are you trying to tell me it was love at first sight?' Even as she said it her heart gave a little thump of excitement.

Pietro was her husband so they must have fallen in love. Yet innate caution, or perhaps the sense that he held back in some way, made her hesitate. On the face of it they seemed an unlikely couple. A rich, sexy Italian businessman and an Aussie teacher-cum-au pair who looked merely average.

Pietro's mouth tucked up at one side in a grin that did something strange to her insides. Her temperature notched up a few degrees and her pulse quickened.

'Love takes more time.' His smile widened to a hungry grin. 'But definitely lust at first sight.'

His expression changed; his gaze snared hers. Heat ignited low in her belly and whooshed upwards like a silent flame engulfing her body. Her skin drew tight, all the fine hairs on her body standing erect as a shiver of animal excitement skittered down her spine.

Common sense told her the woman she'd seen in the mirror wasn't the sort to inspire instant lust in a man like him. She looked pleasant enough, but...

'You don't believe me?' He must have read her expression.

Molly shrugged and took a sip of her cooling drink. 'I'm surprised, that's all.'

His gaze rested on her, considering. 'You don't think you do instant lust?'

Of course she did. The way her body responded to him made that obvious.

'Believe me, it was absolutely mutual.' His voice dropped to a seductive, raspy note that made her shiver and her nipples pucker.

How did he do that with just his voice? No, not just. Those golden eyes shimmered with molten fire and in that instant all her doubts fled. When his gaze ate her up she felt like Venus herself, beautiful and alluring.

'And we got to know each other while I was staying there?'

He nodded. 'You'd bring the children up to the house morning and evening for a swim.'

'It hardly sounds romantic.'

He shrugged. 'We spent time together and got to know each other. I like children and enjoyed their company. And then, when they went to bed early, your evenings were free.' The way he said it, with that throb of inflection, told her those evenings had led to intimacy.

Fire licked her veins and spread through her body.

Abruptly she looked away, breaking the taut connection between them. It seemed both natural to feel this urgent, primal response to her husband, and at the same time unsettling.

Molly took a long swallow of her soft drink, hoping its icy coolness might help dampen the urgent blaze within.

Maybe it would have been easier if he'd wrapped his arms around her and pulled her onto his lap. If he'd showered her with kisses or even just held her hand.

Instead Pietro kept his distance.

He'd said it was because she was an invalid. Surely nothing else could explain his reticence, especially since they were newlyweds? She saw the desire in his eyes.

Molly fought and failed to keep a satisfied smile off her face.

'So sex led to love? I can picture you sweeping a woman off her feet, Pietro.'

'You insist on thinking it was all down to me?' Slowly he shook his head. 'Believe me, I wasn't in the market for a relationship, particularly in my own home. But you made me change my mind.'

Something in his voice scraped at her consciousness. Molly stiffened. The subtle shift in his tone whispered a warning she couldn't interpret.

'You preferred to play the field then walk away?' It made sense. He was broodingly good-looking. She'd bet he only had to snap his fingers for women to come running.

Pietro leaned forward, forearms resting on his thighs. 'I've had lovers, I don't deny it. But that's changed now.' He held her gaze so long she felt her pulse pound three, four, five times, high in her throat. Had any man ever watched her with such intensity?

Frustration rose, for she didn't know even that for certain. She felt like a spectator looking on at her life from the edges. She longed to be able to give in to her attraction for Pietro, to take comfort in the physical side of their relationship. Her body told her it had been both exciting and satisfying.

Yet along with the sexual attraction was a wariness that held her back.

He's still a stranger, even if he's your husband.

She should be grateful he didn't expect her to fall into his arms immediately; that he didn't touch her, but gave her space to feel safe and in control.

Except that control was illusory, wasn't it? She still felt adrift. Pietro's story of them meeting had made her feel better, yet it still prompted more questions than it answered. Who was she? What sort of woman was the real Molly Agosti?

'What was my maiden name?' She didn't even know that!

'Armstrong.' He didn't look fazed by her change of subject. 'You were born Margaret Daisy Armstrong. Apparently you were named after your grandmothers, but you were always called Molly. It's a short form of Margaret.'

She guessed her grandparents weren't alive given her parents weren't. It seemed strange to grieve the loss of people she couldn't recall, yet she did.

'And my sister is Jillian.' It was reassuring to say her name, as if it made her more real. Her sister was her one tangible link with her Australian past. 'How long before she arrives in Rome?'

'I'm sorry.' Pietro spread his hands in an apologetic gesture. 'She's proving hard to locate. She's backpacking around the world, but may have changed her plans and gone to South America before south-east Asia. But I've got people trying to track her down.'

Molly slumped back in her seat, disappointment filling her. She'd counted on seeing Jillian soon. Surely meeting someone with whom she'd shared so much history would finally jog her stubbornly elusive memories?

Strong fingers enfolded hers, holding her gently. She looked up into Pietro's steady gaze.

'It's okay, Molly. We'll find her soon.'

She nodded, overcome by a wave of gratitude that he was here with her, being so understanding.

Now her doubts seemed wrong. Pietro was her husband. He was doing the best he could for her. Clearly he cherished her. Which made her wonder why she was holding back.

'There's something you should know.' She licked her bottom lip, her mouth dry and her heart racing.

'Yes?' He looked like a man not easily fazed, yet how would he react to her news? She wasn't even sure how *she* felt about it.

Molly took a deep breath and hurried on. 'I'm pregnant.'

CHAPTER FIVE

FAMILIAR EXCITEMENT THROBBED through Pietro's chest, the quick pulse of elation making his blood quicken. He met Molly's searching gaze with a smile that held nothing back.

One thing Pietro prided himself on—he never made the same mistake twice. Fate, in the shape of Molly's impaired memory, had given him the chance to replay this crucial moment and get it right second time around.

The first time she'd told him about the pregnancy, after dinner at the Tuscan villa, things hadn't gone well.

Not gone well! It had been an unmitigated disaster. Look where it had got them.

Regret was a sword thrust through his gut. If things had been different, Molly wouldn't have been alone in Rome. There'd have been no accident; no trauma or memory loss.

And he wouldn't be treading a knife edge, waiting for her memory to return. Playing catch-up to bring off the most important coup of his life.

'It's wonderful news. Absolutely wonderful.' He took both her hands in his, feeling them tremble.

'You're not surprised. You knew?'

'I was told earlier.' She'd told him in Tuscany, but he let her think he'd got the news from the hospital staff here in Rome. 'Are you happy about it?'

Slowly she nodded. 'I think so. It's hard to take in. It doesn't seem quite real yet.'

Pietro rubbed his thumb over her wrist, feeling her uneven pulse. 'You've had a lot to contend with. It will take a while to adjust.'

'Were we trying for a child?' Her smile was tentative, almost shy, reminding him that Molly was a complex woman. She had a sunny, easy-going temper, a can-do practical attitude, yet had surprised him with her romanticism.

Molly really did believe in happy endings and true love. That was something he intended to capitalise on.

Pietro's smile grew crooked. He'd known he wanted children but he'd been punctilious about using protection because, after Elizabetta's betrayal, he hadn't been ready to trust another woman. Now the die was cast, he felt a thrill at the idea of a child.

'No, the pregnancy was unexpected. But that doesn't make this child any less a blessing.'

Hearing his response, her high shoulders dropped and he felt her tension lessen.

They weren't hollow words. They came straight from the heart. Hadn't he longed for a family of his own? It was the reason he'd been gulled by Elizabetta all those years ago. Why her cynical manoeuvre had sickened him into avoiding commitment ever since. But Molly wasn't Elizabetta. He understood that now.

'I'm so glad you think like that. I had wondered...'

Pietro lifted her hand to his mouth and pressed his lips to it.

The gesture was meant to be one of comfort and respect. Yet the simple touch of his mouth to her skin, the indefinable, unique taste of her, sent reaction rocketing through him. His hand tightened on hers as something raw and rampant surged to life deep inside him.

Possessiveness.

Molly had run away from him once. It wouldn't happen again. She was the mother of his child and as such her place was with him.

Pietro's voice was rough as he spoke against her hand. 'Never doubt for a moment that I want this child, Molly.' Then he lifted his head, holding her gaze. 'All you have to do for now is concentrate on getting the rest the doctors suggested and try not to worry. Everything will fall into place.'

Two days later Molly dressed with care for dinner. After surveying the rows of restrained, elegant clothes, she'd finally found a short dress in vibrant aqua with narrow shoulder straps and gold beads along the neckline. The colour made her feel confident and happy and the slim-fitting cut made the most of her figure.

Her hand crept to her abdomen. Her pregnancy was only a few weeks along. She didn't feel different physically, and it would be ages before she began to show, but she was determined to make the most of these pretty clothes while she could.

Besides, she had another reason for dressing up tonight.

She put on gold sandals that gave her a few extra

inches and, she decided as she twisted in front of the mirror, showed off her legs.

Would Pietro notice?

Of course he'll notice. He notices everything. The way he looks at you sometimes, it's as if he'd like to eat you up, one tiny bite at a time.

A ripple of excitement coursed through her and deep within Molly registered the liquid heat of desire.

The feeling was familiar and increasingly frequent. And she was sure Pietro felt the same.

Her memory was still a blank, despite the long, restorative sleeps she'd had, but there was nothing wrong with her eyesight. Pietro had a broodingly hot, sexy stare that made her toes curl, though she usually only caught it briefly, when he thought she wasn't looking.

Whenever he kissed her hand, or touched her when he passed food or helped her into a chair, she'd seen the same shock of reaction she felt. It was in his quickened pulse and flared nostrils.

Yet he hadn't done anything about it.

His touch was completely impersonal and platonic.

The only time he'd kissed her had been on the hand, the day they'd talked about the baby and he'd assured her he wanted this child.

Molly had been anxious, not knowing what to expect, and, yes, scared at the prospect of bringing a child into the world when she didn't even know herself. Fortunately Pietro's enthusiasm was contagious. When he spoke of the baby and their future, Molly had no doubt he was excited. She'd begun to believe they'd create a warm, wonderful family. Pietro had been everything she needed—calm and supportive, incredibly caring.

And politely distant.

Damn distant! She wanted feelings. She wanted passion and connection. She wanted intimacy.

Molly wanted to feel alive and real, not like an outsider in her own life.

She was ready to take a plunge and dive back into their relationship. The temptation to do so grew each day. Besides, she needed to break free of this limbo.

She'd been living in a bubble, first in the hospital and then in Pietro's flat.

Molly swallowed hard, banishing the inevitable whisper of distress in her head as the enormity of her loss struck her again. But the doctors were positive. They were confident about the prospects of her memory returning.

Time and again she'd told herself the reason Pietro kept his distance was out of consideration. He knew he must seem like a stranger to her.

Yet he *felt* familiar. The warmth of his hand on hers. The soft gravel of his voice that made the fine hairs on her body stand to attention. The heat in his eyes that evoked an answering fire low in her body.

Molly wanted that and more too. She wanted to feel alive again. She wanted to feel connected, not isolated.

She wanted her husband.

Surely that was proof, if any were needed, that their relationship prior to her memory loss had been strong and passionate?

Tonight she'd find a way to bridge the gap between them.

Pietro was already on the roof terrace when she stepped out into the warm evening. He stood staring out across at the city view, hands thrust in his trouser pockets, his wide shoulders hunched.

Molly halted. It was a rare luxury to observe her husband without him noticing. What she saw intrigued her. There was the stunning profile with the proud, almost arrogant angles of nose and jaw. The lean strength and familiar height was clearly visible beneath the fine tailoring. Yet in repose Pietro didn't look relaxed. His hand in his pocket was fisted and his shoulders looked as though they were drawn tight with tension.

What was bothering him? Business? He'd worked mainly from home since she'd arrived. Was there a problem because he'd neglected work for her? Or was something else tugging down the corners of his mouth?

She crossed the terrace. Molly could have sworn she was quiet enough not to be heard over the sound of water cascading in the fountain and the distant hum of traffic. Yet as she approached Pietro swung round, his eyes meeting hers unerringly.

'*Cara.*' It was a simple endearment, yet it made her needy heart beat faster. 'You look beautiful.'

Molly opened her mouth to voice an automatic denial then snapped it shut. She wasn't used to thinking herself beautiful. That much she *did* know. Yet tonight she felt different, especially seeing the look in Pietro's eyes.

That look propelled her the rest of the way to him. She stopped so close she had to lift her chin up to meet his gaze. The heat of his rangy frame enveloped her and delight shimmered through her as she inhaled the scent of his subtle aftershave. This close she caught a hint of something else—Pietro's own clean, male scent. Her nostrils twitched as she leaned closer.

Instantly he stiffened.

Didn't he like her being so close to him?

Logic told her Pietro kept his distance so as not to rush her, yet doubt instantly took root.

Could there be a rift in their relationship—a problem Pietro didn't like to refer to before her memory returned?

Molly couldn't bear the thought. It might be needy of her, but she wanted their marriage to be strong. It was the only solid thing in her world right now. She'd do whatever it took to make this marriage work, no matter what problems she and Pietro had encountered in the past.

She smiled. 'You look very solemn. What are you thinking about?'

'Nothing much.'

Clearly she was over-sensitive for she imagined steel shutters slamming, making his expression eerily unreadable. Abruptly the heat humming in the air between them dissipated, as if Pietro had flicked a switch.

He'd done that before. Usually he'd talk easily, particularly about their life in Tuscany. But at other times she felt he diverted the conversation, though he explained it by reminding her she shouldn't try to force the memories to return.

'You can talk to me, Pietro. I'm not an invalid any more.' She put her hand on his arm, feeling the warm strength of rigid muscle. 'There's something on your mind, I know. Is it work?'

Slowly his mouth curved and those sexy grooves

dug down through his cheeks, transforming his face from serious to potently attractive.

Being on the receiving end of that smile made the air catch in Molly's lungs. Her fingers wrapped tighter around his arm.

'No. Everything is fine with the business. I told you, I've got efficient managers. I can afford to take a few days away from the office.'

'Then what's bothering you? And don't say it's nothing!' Her voice rose and she clamped her lips, afraid she'd sounded almost shrill. 'If you're worried about me, there's no need. I'm stronger every day.'

'Of course you are.'

Molly clamped her molars in frustration. 'Don't humour me, Pietro.' Great! Now she sounded as if she was spoiling for a fight when nothing could be further from the truth.

Frustrated, she dropped her hand from his arm and turned away to lean on the waist-height terrace wall.

'Molly?'

She didn't turn. Instead she kept her eyes on the rooftops of Rome, washed apricot and amber in the dying sunlight. This was a private oasis, above the city bustle, but despite its beauty and peace Molly needed more. She felt hemmed in by Pietro's unwillingness to share his problems and have a real conversation, and by her physical boundaries.

Shocked, she realised she hadn't left the apartment since coming from the hospital. She'd spent a lot of time sleeping and the rest relaxing with the books Pietro had supplied her with. She'd spent time on the web, looking up places on the east coast of Australia Pietro had said she knew. But still no memories stirred. Maybe that was why she was so antsy.

'Let's go out.' She swung round to find him closer than expected, his expression inscrutable. 'Dinner in a nearby restaurant?'

'Marta is about to serve dinner. But if you want—'

'No, no. I'd forgotten.' No doubt the housekeeper had spent time and effort creating another culinary triumph for their enjoyment.

'What is it, Molly? You don't seem yourself.'

She chewed her lip rather than blurt out her first thought—that it was fine for him to pry but not for her. That was unfair and ungrateful. But it helped her make up her mind.

Molly's eyes met his. 'You're right, I'm restless. I've been cooped up here too long. I know you're concerned for me and, frankly, until tonight I was feeling too tired to go out.'

'That's easily fixed.' Was that relief in his eyes? 'Let's go out tomorrow. We'll tour some of the city sights. Would you like that?'

See? Nothing was too much trouble. She couldn't ask for a more understanding husband. Except...

'That sounds wonderful, Pietro. I'd love to see Rome with you.'

'But?' One sleek black eyebrow lifted in query. He had an uncanny knack of reading her.

She drew a fortifying breath and linked her hands before her. 'I can't shake the feeling there's something wrong between us.'

Had he stiffened?

'You don't open up about what's on your mind. And you don't—'

'Don't what?' His brow furrowed.

'You don't touch me.' She hadn't meant for it to emerge like a challenge.

His eyes rounded in genuine shock. 'That bothers you? I thought, since you didn't remember me…' He lifted his shoulders in an expressive shrug.

Pietro was right. Logic said she wouldn't welcome the touch of a man she barely knew. Except she *did* know him. Something within her yearned for him. Whenever he smiled at her she lit up inside.

Molly refused to feel embarrassed about being attracted to her own husband. He should be *pleased* she wanted him.

'It would be nice if you didn't treat me like a house guest.' She sucked in a lungful of air. 'For instance, I'd like you to kiss me.'

For a second he was utterly still, as if she'd shocked him. Then gold flared in his hooded eyes.

'*That's* what's bothering you? That I haven't kissed you?'

Molly's chin rose and her hands slid to her hips. Pietro didn't smile but she just knew he was laughing inside. She'd never been more certain of anything.

'I don't see the humour.' This wasn't funny! She was tempted to turn away and leave him to his amusement. Except she'd be back to exactly where she'd been before.

'It's not just about kisses. It's about the state of our relationship. Are you holding something back from me? There's something not quite right. You…'

Her words ended as Pietro's big hands wrapped round her elbows and pulled her against him. Her breath expelled in a tiny puff of air. Not from the physical force of the action, but from raw shock.

Molly had told herself she was prepared. Didn't she crave intimacy with him? Yet the sensation of Pietro against her, of that wall of hot muscle making every nerve receptor in her body twang into overdrive, was so much *more* than she'd imagined.

Stunned, she looked at that firm mouth just inches away. It was intriguingly sculpted, strong yet sensual, and it curled up in a delicious invitation that made every atom of her needy body sit up and beg.

Molly swallowed hard, all her bravado swamped by the certainty that, as far as kisses went, Pietro was a consummate expert but she…

Thought atrophied as his head lowered and his mouth opened over hers. Electricity jolted through her. That was the only way she could explain the sizzle that drew her skin tight and puckered her nipples against her bra.

Pietro's lips were softer than she expected, gentle, moving with aching slowness over hers as if taking time to relearn what must surely be familiar territory. Familiar to him. To her this caress felt shockingly new and unfamiliar. His mouth moved again, his tongue licking the seam of her lips, and something drove hard and fast down through her belly straight to that achingly hollow place between her legs.

Molly trembled and grabbed Pietro's arms. She felt the power of them, taut with restraint. He held himself utterly still but for the tantalising slide of lips and tongue.

Another caress, this time more insistent, and something inside her gave way, yielded, yet at the same time blossomed into life.

Molly's lips opened and Pietro's tongue swept deep.

Her knees caved so abruptly it was only his hold that stopped her crashing to the floor. The effect of that deep, searching kiss was instant and overwhelming. Her blood fizzed as every neuron in her brain ignited.

This was what she wanted. What she knew and craved.

Her hands slid high, over hard shoulders and a strong neck, fingers threading through Pietro's thick hair to clamp his skull and hold him to her.

She'd wanted a memory back and now she had it. Not a recollection as such but a sense memory. Her body sparked with excitement and recognition at the taste of him, the heady power of his possession, the familiarity of his hard body pressed against hers.

A sob of relief and arousal rose at the back of her throat as she pushed closer.

That was when the kiss changed, from slow and searching, as if Pietro believed he needed to entice her into a response, to something more potent and urgent.

One large hand anchored on her buttock, drawing her up to his groin. The other cupped her waist, the splay of his fingers hot as a brand through the thin fabric of her dress. It made her wonder how his touch would feel on bare skin.

The notion notched her need higher. Molly opened her mouth wider, stroking his tongue with hers, inviting him to devour her. And all the time a lavish, molten heat swept through her, coalescing in a swirling vortex right at her centre.

Pietro's hand slid up from her waist, his long fingers slipping over first one rib then another, till his thumb brushed the underside of her breast and she sucked in a raw gasp.

That felt so good. On tiptoe now, she tried to merge her body with his, desperate to meld with him.

When his hand closed fully over her breast a jolt of energy zapped from her nipple to her toes, setting off explosions along the way, especially between her legs.

Molly moaned and held on tight as Pietro and her own needy body led her into a sensual world of give and take, of building ecstasy.

A tiny part of her brain screamed that she needed to be careful, to think before she gave herself to him so unstintingly. But she couldn't stop or pull back. She didn't want to. This was a rainbow of colour after a world of grey, delicious food after nothing but ashes in her mouth. It was life, sex and love after fear, pain and loneliness.

How could she resist?

Molly had no idea of resistance. What would she be resisting anyway? Nothing but herself and her own need for affirmation, for life and love.

Hands tight against his scalp, her mouth fused with his, her heart singing, Molly curved her body towards Pietro. To her delight she discovered that he was just as affected. High against her belly pressed a ridge of male arousal. That sign of his matching need was more reassuring even than his gentle words. It was proof positive that, despite everything, the passion and connection they'd shared was still strong.

His primal reaction made her feel powerful, for

the first time since she woke in the hospital. No longer a victim.

But it did more too.

In her few short days of memory, Molly had never been more certain of anything than that Pietro was the man who held her heart. He was the one she'd trusted with her body and her love. For surely it was love, not merely lust, that inundated her, battering aside the fragile protective barriers she'd erected?

It tasted like love. It felt like love, swelling up from the very heart of her.

Molly smiled against her husband's mouth and held on tight as he bent her back over his arm, his mouth hungry on hers, his body thrumming with a barely leashed need that was unmistakable. It was an overt display of masculine strength and possession, and she revelled in it.

Molly slipped one hand down his hard frame to his erection. It was long and every bit as impressive as—

Pietro broke their kiss, head rearing back, dragging her hands from him.

It was only his grip that kept her upright when she wobbled on weakened knees.

Molly blinked, having trouble surfacing from that heady sensual onslaught. His wide chest heaved and the pulse at his throat beat double quick, just like hers.

As she fought to suck oxygen into starved lungs her gaze climbed slowly higher. Past that sensual mouth, now set in a firm line. Past flared nostrils. Up to eyes that blazed more gold than brown.

He looked like a man who wrestled for control. The sight of his struggle pleased her. What if he'd been unmoved? The idea was unbearable. But Pietro had been so controlled, so carefully distant these past few days, that Molly had wondered.

'Why did you stop?'

His straight eyebrows shot up. 'I promised to look after you, Molly, help you recover. But that kiss was headed straight—'

'I know where it was headed, Pietro. I've lost my memory of specifics, not life in general.' The way he'd held back shouldn't chafe so but she was tired of being treated as an invalid. 'There's nothing wrong with a kiss between husband and wife.' She reached out and put her palm flat to his chest, registering the heavy throb of his heartbeat, only marginally slower than her own.

'With Marta about to serve dinner?' She was surprised at the frown marking his brow.

Surely a kiss was no big deal?

Yet Pietro looked strangely out of sorts as he lifted his hand and speared his fingers through his hair. It was perfectly cut, falling back into place instantly, gleaming black against his olive skin and the golden glow of his signet ring.

Something jerked hard in Molly's chest. She stiffened.

Pietro dropped his hand to his side and her gaze followed the movement.

Her forehead puckered in concentration. Something hovered, just beyond her consciousness. Some vital thing she needed to...

'Molly? What is it?'

She shook her head, snatching desperately at the wisp of... Was it a memory?

'I don't know. There's something...something I've

almost remembered.' It took everything she had not to look at Pietro, knowing his excitement would feed her own and probably destroy any hope she had of retrieving this tantalising thought.

'Lift your hand again.'

He did so, bringing it palm-up between them.

Molly frowned but there was no nudge of enlightenment.

She took his hand in hers and turned it over, noting the long, capable fingers, the broad back of his hand, olive-skinned with a sprinkling of black hair. Noting the heavy signet ring, the neat nails. He had sexy hands, strong hands. The sort of hands she could imagine skimming and caressing her bare body.

Molly's thumb traced a line across his fingers. Then, barely knowing she did it, she lifted her own hand, staring at it beside Pietro's, noting the difference in size and colouring, in strength and...

Enlightenment was a slash of lightning across her vision, a stab to her heart.

She stumbled back till Pietro caught her, his hands around her shoulders. His hands were steady but she was shaking.

It couldn't be! But she knew what she'd seen. What her brain had finally revealed.

It wasn't memory at all, merely belated logic, and it left her with a sick feeling in the pit of her stomach.

'You can let me go now.' Her voice was clipped as she wrestled with panic.

When Pietro's arms dropped, she stepped back, locking her knees. Desperately she concentrated on dragging air into struggling lungs.

'Is it a memory? You look like you've seen a ghost.'

Her lips curved in a mirthless smile as she stared into that bold, beautiful, lying face. She noticed again the arrogance there as well as the concern. He was right to be worried. It was ridiculous she hadn't worked it out before. Her only excuse was she'd not really been coping with anything much apart from sleeping and minimal exertion.

'No, I haven't remembered anything.'

Expression flickered in his eyes but it was unreadable, as were his features. Pietro, she realised, had a perfect poker face.

'But I finally realised something I should have noticed straight away.' She grabbed his hand and raised it between them. 'You wear a signet ring.'

Slowly he nodded. 'It was my father's. It means a lot to me.'

'More than your marriage? You don't wear a wedding ring.'

Molly knew she was right by the way his mouth tightened, tiny lines bracketing the corners. His jaw set hard, as if he bit back a response.

'Of course, not all men wear wedding bands, but most Australian women do.' How she knew for sure was beyond her, but Molly had no doubt she was right. '*I'd* wear a ring if I were married. And yet...' she lifted her hand to show him '...there's no ring. Nor a mark to show I used to wear one.'

Why hadn't she realised sooner? It was such a simple thing. Should she blame her poor, confused brain for being slow? Or had she allowed herself to be gulled because she'd wanted so much to believe in Pietro, in *them*? Had she subconsciously decided not to question his version of events too hard because she'd wanted so badly to belong somewhere?

She dropped her hand and took another step backwards, aware of the dormant strength of the big man before her and the fact that he'd lied to her about such an important thing.

Suddenly his strength seemed threatening rather than comforting. Her spine iced as she fought panic.

'We're not married, are we, Pietro? What do you want from me?' Her voice rose. 'Why am I here?'

CHAPTER SIX

MOLLY HAD EXPECTED a reaction. Dismay, perhaps, or embarrassment at being caught lying. Something.

Instead she looked into Pietro's face and read nothing at all.

For a split second she wondered if she'd got it wrong. If, despite her surmises, they were married after all. But the dead stillness of his expression told her she was right. Now he waited to see how she would react.

He'd been prepared for this moment.

'I'm sorry, Molly.'

She heard regret in his soft voice and it made the hair on her arms stand on end. Abruptly the balmy evening turned chilly. She rubbed her hands up her bare arms, trying to get warm. Trying to stimulate her circulation, which seemed to have frozen.

No denial, then.

Her heart sank as anxiety tore through her. It was true. Pietro Agosti wasn't her husband.

Who was he? Someone who preyed on vulnerable women?

But then why had he broken that kiss when he could so easily have…? No, she refused to follow that line of thought.

Was she a prisoner here?

Her eyes darted past him, measuring the distance into the apartment and then to the front door. If she had to run for it she'd have no hope. His long legs would cover the distance far more quickly.

Why had he claimed to be her husband? Her mind whirled so fast she didn't have time to grab at any logical explanation. Her breathing grew short and stress made her dizzy.

'Take a deep breath.' His voice was low and even, like someone talking to a scared child. He stepped back and pulled a chair forward. 'Here. You've had a shock.'

Molly swayed, but refused to obey. She stiffened her knees.

'Don't tell me what to do!' There was no way she could sit and have him loom over her. 'As for a shock, whose fault is that?' Finding refuge in anger, she crossed her arms and glared at him, pretending to be furious instead of furious and frightened.

Who was this man who'd abducted her and brought her to his home? More to the point, who was *she*? Were those stories he'd told about their time together, her background, even her name, all false, just like their so-called marriage?

Terror welled deep inside but she pretended not to notice, choosing to concentrate on anger.

'If you're not my husband, who are you? Why did you bring me here?'

'I'm Pietro Agosti, as I told you.' His look was steady, as if he expected her to take his word.

'Why should I believe you?'

He drew a wallet out of his pocket and withdrew

an identification card: Pietro Agosti, thirty-two, with an address in Rome. He passed over a couple of credit cards in the same name.

Molly's thundering heart slowed a fraction. So he'd told her his real name. 'This says you live in Rome, not Tuscany.'

He shrugged and spread his hands in a gesture of openness she refused to believe. 'I spend time between them. This is my official residence. The Tuscan villa is my family home, inherited from my parents.'

Her fingers closed around the cards as she looked up into shuttered eyes.

'Believe me, I did it for the best. There was no way the hospital staff would tell me about your condition, or release you into my care, unless they believed we were married. It was a necessary ruse, otherwise you'd still be stuck there, alone and fretting. They had to believe I was your next of kin.'

She heard urgency in his voice, earnestness, but didn't trust either. How could she? Even his ID card, cutting into her curling fist, didn't prove much.

'I was sick with worry, Molly. I *had* to see you were all right.' At last, a glimpse of emotion in those hooded eyes.

Was it real or feigned? Her heart hammered and, despite the chill in her bones, her skin turned clammy. She didn't know what to believe.

'The trouble was, once I'd told the hospital we were married, I couldn't unsay it. I've been wondering when to tell you the truth without distressing you. You'd remember eventually but who knew how long that would take?' Pietro's shoulders lifted high as once more he gestured wide, his mouth hitching in a crooked smile that caught at her midriff. Instinct told her she'd responded to that deprecating half-smile before.

Because he'd duped her more than once?

Or because he was, after all, trustworthy?

'There never seemed a good time to explain. You still seemed...delicate. I didn't think you were ready for the truth.'

'But not too delicate to kiss!' Molly repressed a shudder as she wrapped her arms tighter around her middle.

Who had she kissed? What of her certainty that she responded to Pietro because they were lovers? Had she come on to a complete stranger who, for his own devious purposes, kept her here?

What of her glorious feeling of homecoming? What of shared passion and love? Were they simply the illusions of a damaged mind?

She was a fool, a trusting, stupid fool.

'Ah, I should apologise for that too.' Yet instead of apologising Pietro smiled. The glow of satisfaction in his face made her insides squeeze and her knees tremble. 'I should have resisted, but a man only has so much restraint.'

'Because I'm at your mercy?' It was a sickening thought, despite her body's response to him.

His eyes bulged in horror and that satisfied smile vanished. 'Because you're my lover!'

'I am?'

'Of course! Why else would I scour Rome for you?'

'I only have your word for that.'

Pietro's head jerked back as if she'd slapped him. His eyes narrowed and she saw his mind working.

'You think—what? That I'm a complete stranger

who walked into the hospital off the street, looking for a woman to prey on? That I brought you home, bought you a wardrobe of clothes and tried to look after you because I had some underhanded plan for you?' His proud nostrils flared and his jaw clenched as if he'd never been so insulted.

Let him be insulted! She needed answers.

Molly angled her chin, meshing her gaze with his. 'I don't know what to think. I've just discovered the one person in the world who claims to know anything about me has been lying. All I know about you is your name.' Her hands crept to her hips as she fought to keep her tone even. 'What am I supposed to believe? I don't know anything. Not even if I can trust you.'

Tension was a twanging, discordant note reverberating through her body. It was nausea in her stomach and the bitter taste of fear on her tongue. It took everything Molly had to stand there and meet him head on.

Pietro muttered something under his breath and spun away in a long-legged march down the length of the terrace. She heard soft swearing in Italian as he stalked back. He stopped several paces away, his hand raking his scalp, shoulders hitched high.

'I'm sorry, Molly.' His voice was as stiff. 'I knew finding out the truth would be a shock but I never imagined you'd think anything like *that*.'

He moved to the half-wall on the edge of the terrace, gripping it so tightly his knuckles paled.

'First, you're absolutely safe with me. I'm not a criminal or a sex fiend.'

Molly opened her mouth to say she only had his word for that, but snapped it shut. Better to let him speak then ask questions.

'I can get references if you like.' Again that tiny twist of his lips that did funny things to her insides. 'I know a couple of judges and a senior police officer—would they do?'

Molly shrugged. How would she know if they were who he said?

'Second, you really are Molly Armstrong from Australia, and we met just the way I told you.'

Relief gushed through her. She wanted to believe him so much, not least because the idea of becoming once more that nameless woman without a past was too much to bear.

'And we are lovers. I thought after that kiss there'd be no doubt in your mind but this might help.' He reached in his pocket and drew out a phone.

'What is that?'

'A photo of us.'

Molly's eyebrows rose. They'd talked and talked about her past but she hadn't thought to ask about photos. The knock to her head really had affected her! 'Why didn't you show it to me before?'

His eyes met hers. 'Because I didn't want you asking for more photos—of our wedding, for instance.'

Because he'd lied and there'd been no wedding.

But maybe, just maybe, they were in a relationship and he'd been desperate to see her in the hospital. And, having seen her in hospital, he'd realised how desperate *she* was to get out of there.

'Here.' He handed over his phone. It was a selfie Pietro had taken. He was shirtless, squatting in front of an aquamarine pool in swim shorts. For a second Molly's attention dawdled on the expanse of taut muscle on display. Then she saw herself in a black bikini, her hair in drenched rats' tails and smile wide. Between them was a grinning little boy with brown hair and glasses.

Molly's heart thudded, her eyes widening as she looked for facial similarities.

'Who…?'

'That's Tom, one of your charges. He wanted a photo.'

Molly stared at the image, taking in their relaxed attitude and wide smiles. And Pietro's fingers clamped on her bare waist.

She shivered, envisaging his hand on her, how it felt to snuggle up against all that solid muscle and sinew.

Then Pietro's words hit her. Tom had wanted a photo. Not Pietro. Was that significant? Pietro claimed they were lovers, and this photo seemed to bear that out, but it was nothing like proof. Surely a lover would have a photo of her?

'Do you have any other photos of us?'

He stilled, reading her expression. 'Just a moment.' He thumbed his way through more photos then passed the phone back to her.

Molly barely recognised the woman in the photo. She lay barefoot on a blanket spread beneath the gnarled trunk of an olive tree. Her skirt was rucked up around her knees and the top buttons of her lacy camisole-style top were undone, revealing a shadowed cleavage. But it wasn't her rumpled clothes that snagged her attention. It was her beckoning smile of invitation as she held a bunch of purple grapes to her lips and the sultry, heavy-lidded stare she directed straight at the camera.

Heat flushed her breasts and throat as she stared at her alter ego. Molly couldn't quite believe she could pull off such a sexy, confident look.

Unless she was in love.

The tiny voice in her head jarred. But it made sense. Either she was head over heels in love with the man who took the photo or that was pure lust she read in her body language. Either way, it pointed to a level of intimacy that explained why she'd leaned so close to Pietro in the previous photo.

'I…see.' She didn't know what to say.

Strangely she felt like a voyeur peering into someone else's love life, for she couldn't remember a thing about their relationship.

Except that it had felt so right being in his arms. So perfect when his mouth fused with hers and he hauled her high against him.

Instinct had been right after all. She'd yearned for Pietro because they were lovers, or had been lovers.

Slowly she lifted her head. Pietro's gaze fixed unwaveringly on her. 'Now you understand why our kiss was so explosive.'

Molly started. It really was as if he'd read her mind!

'Don't deny it, Molly. I was there too. I felt it.' He smiled, that slow smile that turned the blood in her veins to honey and her knees to limp ribbons of pasta. 'Even without your memory we still connect.' He didn't bother to hide his satisfaction. Who could blame him? She hadn't merely participated, she'd all but demanded he kiss her. 'That was a relief.'

'Sorry?' Had she missed something?

His shoulders rose in a deprecating gesture. 'I didn't think, with your memory gone, you'd want to kiss me. Yet you did, and it was just the same between us. Just as powerful.'

There was a golden glint in his eyes that spoke of…anticipation?

Instantly Molly stepped back, recognising something primal and predatory in that look.

It was one thing to crave comfort from her husband, but she didn't yet know where she stood with Pietro. They'd been lovers, that seemed clear. Were they still?

Yet she couldn't fathom any reason why he'd lie about that.

'The baby!' How could she have forgotten? Her hand pressed protectively to her abdomen. 'Is it…?'

'It's mine. Don't doubt that for a second.' The hint of a smile playing around Pietro's lips vanished, his look turning serious. He stepped closer, just an arm's length away. This time Molly didn't move back, though she felt unsettled by his invasion of her personal space, as if he projected a force field that detonated warnings all through her jangled senses.

'Or, I should say, it's *our* child.' His voice was pure caress. 'We'll be raising it together.'

'We will?' What had she agreed to? Some sort of long-distance shared parenting? Or had she agreed to stay in Italy?

'Of course.' He bestowed one of those smiles on her that made her knees rock and her insides melt. 'We're getting married.'

'We're engaged?' Molly's hand lifted to her throat as if to stop the fluttering sensation where her heart beat high.

Why was the idea so shocking? Half an hour ago she'd thought them already married.

Maybe it was because of the sheer greedy satisfaction she read in Pietro's face. He didn't bother hiding his feelings now and she was overwhelmed by the intensity of his pleasure. Because he couldn't wait to marry her?

Molly's pulse pounded and an answering excitement built deep within.

It was a powerful thing to be so wanted.

Her heart seized as he took her hand in his. He kissed it, not on the back this time, but her palm, making tiny threads of delight unravel up her arm, across her shoulders and down her spine.

Her visceral response to Pietro told her she longed for him too, especially on a physical level.

And what of the rest? Are you just going to accept everything he says? Didn't he lie about being married? But was that only so he could bring you home?

Molly looked into Pietro's proud face and wanted to believe everything was as simple as he said. It probably was. Certainly her response to his touch, even to that heavy-lidded stare, told her she craved this man.

Yet she knew so little about herself. Let alone him.

She looked at her hand in his.

'I've only got your word for it that we're engaged.'

Pietro nodded, releasing her.

'Will you excuse me for a moment? I have something that should clear that up.' Then he was gone, striding purposefully across the darkening terrace. In the doorway he met the housekeeper and said something to her. Was he delaying their meal?

Molly turned and sank onto a chair, trying to calm her sprinting pulse with deep breaths and the gorgeous view of Rome spread out before her.

What was she to believe? Pietro seemed so plausible. Certainly she felt safe with him, and he'd clearly gone to a lot of trouble to look after her. The idea of him providing character references made her smile, but maybe she should follow that up.

Except her heart told her there was no need. Her heart made it clear Pietro was important to her. Not only as the man who'd rescued her from that grey hospital room but as the man she cared for.

Did she love him?

It was tempting to believe so. But one thing Molly had learned in the past few days—to take things slowly and assume nothing.

If only she could remember something. Anything!

So far her memory consisted of two things: her tendency to kill more plants than she grew, and a sense memory of being held by Pietro, losing herself in his kiss. Thinking about that ignited flames low inside.

Her mouth turned down and familiar fear battered her resolve not to crumple. Surely soon there'd be a breakthrough? Or at least another snippet of the past. Then another and another. She just had to be patient.

Molly shook her head, her hair slipping around her shoulders. She didn't even know if she was a patient woman! She could ask Pietro but could she really trust him? She wished her sister Jillian were here.

Footsteps sounded on the paving stones and she turned to watch Pietro cross the roof garden. In the early evening light he looked like a female fantasy of tall, dark and handsome made flesh. As he drew near those piercing eyes glowed with a warmth that tangled her thoughts.

'I've been keeping this safe for you.' He held out a small, square, blue velvet box.

Molly's heart catapulted against her ribs. Her breath snatched as butterflies wheeled and spun in her stomach.

'What is it?' She had a good idea but for some reason wasn't in a rush to touch his hand and take the box.

'It's yours.'

Molly swallowed hard. Reaching out to take that box felt like crossing a boundary. Yet she had to see.

The velvet was warm from Pietro's hand. She paused, holding it for a moment, then opened the lid. Fire dazzled up at her, flaring and shifting as her hand trembled. The butterflies dancing inside her became kites, swirling so fast she felt dizzy.

It was a ring, of course. A dazzling statement piece that would take any woman's breath away.

'It's an opal.' Not just any opal. The gem was indigo-blue with traceries of iridescent green and, when she turned it, flashes of red appeared as if from some inner fire. 'It's utterly gorgeous.' And that was without the ring of diamonds circling the large centre stone.

Molly's eyes widened. This must have cost a fortune! Her gaze slewed to Pietro and found him smiling down at her. 'I'm pleased you think so. I thought you'd like something from your homeland.'

The thoughtfulness of that brought a lump to Molly's throat. It was the action of a man who truly cared. A man concerned that she might miss her own country.

'It's your engagement ring.' He paused, a tiny frown

gathering on his brow. 'I didn't have a chance to give it to you before. I'd like to see you wear it.'

There was no doubting Pietro's sincerity. That expectant look made him appear for the first time something other than confident and in control. As if everything rode on her accepting the gift.

Just like any other man, waiting to see if his fiancée approved his choice of ring.

The realisation touched her. Had she made a mountain out of a mole hill, worrying about Pietro claiming they were married when he'd simply wanted to see her and bring her home?

'When did you—?'

'When did I get the ring? I ordered it when I was in Tuscany. It was made to my specifications.'

In Tuscany. He'd ordered this precious thing but it hadn't arrived before she'd come to Rome, which was why she hadn't been wearing it when she'd woken in hospital. They couldn't have been engaged long.

'You said we met only a few months ago. It's not long to get to know someone before becoming engaged.'

His look made her blood sizzle. 'Long enough, Molly. I know you're the woman I want to marry.' His tone rang with absolute certainty and her needy heart weakened.

He paused, obviously waiting for her to say something. But words failed her. No matter what had gone before, how could she speak of love and marriage when she barely knew him?

When she didn't respond Pietro went on, his brow knitting in a frown, a pulse ticking at his temple. 'You wanted marriage too. That's what you said.'

Molly didn't miss the past tense. Is that why Pietro seemed so tense? Despite his smile his expression was tight. His stillness told her he was on edge. Was he waiting for her to declare she still felt the same?

Anxiety trickled through her, and a hint of excitement.

Pietro looked almost stern as he waited for her response, as if it was difficult to harness patience.

'It's stunning, Pietro, and I want to wear it. But I feel…odd. I can't remember being engaged to you and…' To her mortification, tears crowded her eyes, threatening to spill as she stared up at him. Her emotions see-sawed horribly.

'Shh, Molly. It's okay.' Pietro pulled her to him and wrapped his arms around her. 'There's nothing to be upset about. This can wait. The important thing is you know how things stand.'

She shook her head against his collarbone, feeling almost guilty about taking solace in his embrace when she couldn't bring herself to put on the ring. 'I'm just overwhelmed. It's so lovely, and you've gone to such trouble, but I don't remember anything about us and it seems wrong to accept it when I can't.'

His chin rested on her head, one hand stroking her hair, the other splayed at her back.

'Don't fret. As for not recalling us, that will change.' He pulled back just enough to look down at her, tilting her face towards his. 'Relax, Molly. Keep the ring and wear it when it feels right.' He favoured her with a smile that she felt all the way to her toes and made her wonder why she was holding back. 'Let's forget that for now. Come on, dinner is being served.'

His warm hand closed around hers and he led her to the pergola with its perfumed vines. Beneath it the table had been set for two with linen and silverware. Fat candles flickered, casting a gentle glow.

But as the meal progressed it was Pietro's solicitude that made the evening romantic.

He ignored the ring box she placed on the table and kept her amused with stories about Rome and sightseeing plans.

As the time passed Molly relaxed. How many men in Pietro's situation would have been so forbearing? Clearly he cared about her. There'd been no mistaking his urgency as he'd waited for her to accept the ring. Yet he was willing to wait till she was comfortable with him.

She was lucky to have such a man in her life.

Pietro watched Molly's rigid posture relax, read the pleasure in her eyes and knew he'd been right not to push.

No matter how frustrating it was to wait. Tension clamped his neck and jaw and he had to make an effort not to let it show.

Her distress tonight hit home. Seeing her scared and worried evoked latent protective instincts. That moment when she'd realised they weren't married…

He'd acted on impulse, claiming to be her husband, only realising later that she must notice at some point that she had no wedding ring. By then it had been too late—the deed was done. Besides, when Molly wore his wedding band it would be for real, not a sham simply to get her out of hospital.

As for their engagement… Pietro needed to move

slowly. If he forced the matter he might frighten her away and then he'd be right back to square one.

His belly clenched at the memory of her walking out of his villa in Tuscany. Not, as she currently believed, for a short holiday in Rome. But because she'd been stopping briefly in Rome before catching her flight to Australia with no plans ever to return.

They hadn't bid each other a fond, lingering farewell. He'd been rigid with fury and Molly had said she never wanted to see him again. Then she'd angled her nose in the air and strode out, the picture of hauteur, despite her swimming eyes.

A pang of remorse opened a chasm in his belly.

It was true he'd ordered the engagement ring while at the villa. Not because he'd proposed and she'd accepted, but because she'd only been gone a few hours when he'd realised his mistake.

They *would* marry. He could *not* relinquish his unborn child. Family was everything. It was not merely important but something he'd craved almost as long as he could remember. Ever since his own family had been so cruelly ripped away from him. Even now he felt the old, secret yearning, the bleak, emptiness at the centre of his world that no amount of success could ever fill.

The solution was easy. Ensure custody of his child by binding Molly to him in marriage.

After all, she'd looked at him with stars in her eyes when she'd told him about the pregnancy the first time. Her tentative references to a possible future together had betrayed her romantic hopes.

A rusty blade knifed his ribs as he watched Molly

smile at him from across the table. So sweet, yet still so tentative.

Just as well she couldn't remember their last evening in Tuscany.

For the first time since Elizabetta, the first time in six years, Pietro had let emotion overtake logic in a devastating tsunami that had obliterated sense. His blood ran cold as he recalled what he'd said to Molly that night.

No time to think of that now. He needed to focus on the present. And the all-important future, when he'd have the family he'd always longed for.

He just had to secure it.

Molly smiled again, gesturing to emphasise a point. When she put her hand down, Pietro reached out and covered it with his. He felt her stiffen, felt her pulse race beneath that silky skin. Her eyelids flickered and she looked away but she didn't slide her hand free.

Pietro suppressed his smile. He knew it would be triumphant and he couldn't risk signalling his feelings.

Molly was a romantic. She'd fallen like a ripe cherry into his hand and his bed before. And she'd been ready to fall into marriage.

All he had to do was court her and get her to fall for him again. Seduce her.

That way, when her memory returned there'd be no nonsense about them parting. He'd have her where he wanted her—in his home, bringing up his child.

Pietro loved a simple, fool-proof plan.

CHAPTER SEVEN

THE NEXT DAY was tiring but good.

So very good. Molly couldn't stop smiling. She hadn't realised what a difference it would make to be out and about in the city. Pietro's apartment was spacious and designer-attractive, and the views were wonderful, but she'd begun to feel hemmed in. This was her first real outing since waking in that sterile hospital room.

Hurriedly she yanked her thoughts away from the place back to the present. This felt like freedom.

Pietro cut a glance her way. 'Ready to sit for a while?'

'That sounds ideal. Thank you.'

His eyes were hidden by reflective sunglasses, so she couldn't read his expression, but he nodded and guided her towards an outdoor café. She had the impression that he was carefully attuned to her needs. All day he'd been laid back but unobtrusively solicitous, as if knowing how surprisingly fatiguing this first day out would be for her. Not so much from exercise but from being bombarded by all the sights and sounds.

Around them women stared and even turned to watch Pietro, but he seemed oblivious, concentrating only on Molly.

That made her heart flip over and she fought to keep her expression neutral.

He was formidably gorgeous, even down to his designer loafers and trendy button-down shirt.

More than that, he was a perfect companion, attentive and fun, protective when the crowds in some of the tourist hot spots threatened to jostle her. There'd been a moment, as strangers had closed around them, when she'd felt a surge of panic, till Pietro had slid his arm around her and smoothly extricated her from the mob. He hadn't said anything, just diverted her with some amusing anecdote. Yet Molly knew he'd sensed her panic and acted to dispel it.

His unobtrusive care was tantalisingly attractive, as much as his rangy, masculine frame and the rare smile that turned her blood effervescent.

She still didn't know how she felt about Pietro, apart from attracted and too needy for her own good. It would take time to forgive him for that lie about them being married. But today had been a good start. Some of the invisible weight bearing down on her had already eased.

'Thank you, Pietro.' She sat at the tiny vacant table that had miraculously appeared at their approach and leaned towards him.

His eyebrows arched above his sunglasses. 'For what?'

Molly smiled. 'For everything. For today. I know you put off your work to spend time with me.'

She'd heard him early that morning, busy on the phone. One of his many calls had been in English as he'd apologised personally for rescheduling a meeting. He'd said he had to devote himself to an important family matter.

Hearing herself described as 'family' went a long way to settling the riot of nerves she'd felt on discovering they weren't married.

Pietro spread his hands in a familiar gesture. 'Some things are more important than work, Molly.'

There it was again, that tug at the heartstrings when he put her first. Or maybe it was the way he said her name with that sexy, lilting accent, making it sound as delicious as the *gelato* he'd bought her earlier.

'I appreciate it. I suspect visiting tourist sites isn't the norm for you.' For one thing his style was far more sophisticated than that of the average tourist.

Pietro took off his glasses and fixed her with a look that suffused her with warmth. 'You haven't been to Rome before. Not properly. Of course you want to see some of the famous sites. Sharing your enjoyment has been a great pleasure. Thank *you*. I feel privileged.'

His mouth tilted up in the merest hint of a smile and her stomach went into freefall.

So much for her determination to take things slowly and not be swayed by attraction.

With an effort she dragged her gaze away, taking in the crowd thronging the *piazza*.

'What would you like?' Pietro's words interrupted her thoughts.

'Oh.' She'd been so busy thinking about Pietro she hadn't noticed the waiter appear. 'Not coffee.' She frowned down at the menu she hadn't even opened. It was late in the afternoon, and some of the other café patrons sipped beer or wine, but she was avoiding alcohol. 'A soft drink with lots of ice, please.'

Pietro ordered then turned back to her. 'I'm glad you enjoyed the Pantheon.'

'Oh, I did. It was just as wonderful as I'd hoped.' She turned to stare at the huge domed building on the other side of the square, still not quite believing it. 'To go inside an ancient Roman building was amazing, especially one so imposing. And that wide hole in the roof!' She shook her head. 'I read about it and wondered what happened when it rained but I hadn't realised there were drains under the floor to take the water away. Silly of me, wasn't it? It wasn't what I expected.'

She looked back to find Pietro watching her curiously.

'What did you expect?'

'Something smaller. But walking between those enormous columns at the entrance made me feel totally insignificant. You really could feel the age of it. We don't have such old buildings in Australia. The oldest one I've been in is Cadman's Cottage in Sydney. Built in the early nineteenth century.'

Pietro's eyes narrowed. 'When did you read about the Pantheon? In the apartment?'

'No, I...' Molly's eyes widened as she met his.

He nodded. 'I thought so, when you started talking. It wasn't in the last few days, was it, Molly? You remembered reading about it before you came to Italy, or at least before arriving in Rome.'

'Before the accident.' She breathed in a wispy voice as her throat tightened. She could picture it now—not a screen but a book, some sort of travel guide with a photo of the Pantheon's huge interior taking up a double-page spread. She saw herself turning the page, seeing the Colosseum, the Spanish Steps, art galleries, *piazzas* and bright-blue skies.

She swallowed hard, an odd feeling making her flesh tingle and draw tight. 'It's a memory.' It was both scary and exciting. 'I thought I'd remember the important things first, like you, or my family.' Molly lifted her eyes to Pietro.

Surprisingly he didn't look excited, but more wary, as if wondering what she'd reveal next.

Who could blame him? It must be like walking on eggshells, wondering how she'd react. Again it hit her that he really *had* been wonderful, uncomplaining and considerate.

'More than one memory, Molly.'

'You mean the one about me gardening?' Her pulse quickened. 'That's two things in two days.'

'Three. You just mentioned a place you've visited in Australia. A cottage in Sydney. It wasn't just that you knew about it, you knew you'd visited it.'

Molly felt her stare grow fixed as she gazed into his golden-brown eyes. Pietro was right. It *was* another memory. Warm shivers trickled over her skin as she pictured herself walking from the water at Circular Quay in Sydney across the open space to the neat stone cottage.

She could feel the breeze off the harbour cooling the back of her neck as she herded a group of small children towards the cottage. Nearby another teacher, an older woman, flashed a weary smile as she counted their charges.

Molly heard the echo of a cheer at the promise of ice-creams later, and then a cry as little Sally Paynton tripped and grazed her knee.

She frowned, trying to hold onto the image, the clarity of the moment, yet even as she did so it wavered and faded. The memory dissolved, leaving her mouth dry and her heart thumping.

Warmth stole through her and she blinked, lifting her head to see Pietro's concerned face. Something caressed her hand and she realised it was his thumb brushing her wrist, his fingers warming hers.

Molly felt like a diver coming back to the surface of the sea, disorientated. Yet Pietro didn't rush her with questions. He merely waited, his touch gentle yet proprietorial and, she realised with a start, an expression on his face that looked implacable. As if he was readying himself to fight some demon on her behalf.

What worrying recollections did he think might surface? Or was that simply her disturbed brain inventing things?

'You're right.' She turned her hand and squeezed his. 'I remembered visiting there with a school group. It was hot and the kids were tired and one of them fell over.' She paused as the significance of that recollection struck. 'I even recall her name—Sally Paynton!'

'*Brava, tesoro*. That's amazing. Your memory is starting to work again. That must be such a relief.'

Pietro couldn't know how much. 'It's true. I'd begun to fear I might never recover.' She'd avoided admitting it. The fear ran so deep, mentioning it was like tempting fate.

His hand tightened on hers, imbuing her with warmth and reassurance. 'And now you know you were wrong.'

So simple, yet so decisive. With those few words Pietro banished the horror that lurked in the silent night hours. 'You're right. I may not get everything back, but there'll be more to come, I'm sure of it.'

The waiter arrived, bearing a tray of drinks and snacks. With a flourish he put down their glasses, a frosted glass for her and a wine glass for Pietro, then a platter of bread and *antipasto*.

Pietro raised his glass in a toast, still keeping hold of her other hand. 'To you, Molly.' He paused, then added, 'And to our future together.'

A thud of heat pulsed through her as she read his look. Approval and possessiveness. Both gleamed bright and unmistakable in that searing stare.

Molly told herself she wasn't ready for anything more than friendship, not till she got her mind working again. But her body wouldn't co-operate. She couldn't even find the energy to tug her hand free. Detonations exploded along her nerve endings. Her breasts tingled and swelled, her flesh tightening as something slid sideways deep inside.

Not simply because Pietro looked at her like a lover.

But because she wanted him to be just that.

She waited for doubt to assail her. But instead she felt only a sense of rightness. It was as if her body recognised and accepted Pietro while her brain struggled to catch up. Was she crazy, trying to hold back from him? With every moment it became clearer that he was incredibly important to her.

At the last moment innate wariness intervened. 'To the future.' Silently she acknowledged she wanted theirs to be a joint future, even if she wasn't ready to commit to that yet.

Far from being annoyed at her amended toast, Pietro squeezed her hand and smiled lazily. As if he had all the time in the world for her to accept him, accept *them.* That, more than anything else, settled the last of her doubts and made her grin back at him.

Maybe everything would be all right after all.

'Pietro!' A young woman, slim and vibrant in tight jeans and a bright top, emerged from the crowd. She embraced Pietro, kissing him on both cheeks and bursting into animated Italian.

Molly stiffened and tried to prise her hand free, but Pietro's grip stayed firm. Her mouth turned down as she surveyed the vivacious stranger who was clearly intimate with Pietro.

Molly registered a curious, curdling sensation in her stomach as she watched the pretty stranger monopolise him.

It could *not* be jealousy. The odd feeling was probably due to gulping an icy drink on a hot day. Except, she realised, she hadn't taken a sip.

Molly was frowning over the thought when Pietro extricated himself. 'Chiara, you need to speak English. Molly doesn't speak Italian. Molly, this is my cousin, Chiara.'

'Your cousin?' Molly felt an uprush of relief. Despite what she'd said about taking things slowly, the idea of Pietro being intimate with any other woman had made her feel nauseous.

Because he's yours. Face it. You've wanted him from the moment you saw him in that hospital room. There was a spark, a connection you can't deny.

'Molly? You're a good friend of Pietro's?' Chiara's inquisitive gaze dropped to the table where Pietro's hand enfolded Molly's. For a moment her eyes widened then she grinned and pulled out a chair to sit and lean closer. 'How lovely to meet you, Molly. I'm looking forward to hearing *all* about you and Pietro. Every little detail and—'

'*Adesso basta.*' Pietro shook his head. 'Molly isn't here to entertain you.'

His hand curled tight around Molly's and she felt once more that inner glow. He might be over-protective but he cared. Molly had a strong suspicion she was used to standing up for herself, not relying on a man to protect her. But, in this still alien world, it was comforting to have him so obviously on her side.

'It's nice to meet you, Chiara.' She smiled back at the other woman who looked just a few years younger than her. 'I don't know anything about Pietro's family.'

'You don't?' Perfectly arched ebony eyebrows rose in shock. 'He hasn't told you about his favourite cousin?' Her expression turned to mock dismay as she regarded Pietro.

'Favourite? You mean your brother?' His retort was belied by the humour in his expression.

Chiara shook her head then batted her eyelashes in such an exaggerated way Molly stifled a laugh. 'I mean me, of course. Your devoted cousin.'

'Oh, you mean the one who never stops talking? The one who gets underfoot?'

Chiara's eyes danced. 'Males enjoy attention. It's a proven fact.'

Pietro snorted. 'Do they indeed? And I was supposed to enjoy being badgered constantly about lending you my new car?'

Chiara's smile became a pout. 'Don't tell me you're still going on about that?' She turned to Molly. 'It was a tiny scratch. No more.'

'Tiny?' Pietro's voice was a mock growl.

Molly listened to their banter and wondered if this was how things were between her and Jillian. Meanwhile, it was fun seeing the affection between Pietro and his cousin. It confirmed her impression of him as genuine. A man she could trust. It made a mockery of her fear when she'd learned his lie about them being married.

As for that hovering sense of something shadowy and hidden, something Pietro was keeping from her, surely that was only the imaginings of a fertile mind? She was reading too much into his caution as he attempted to deal with her amnesia.

'Molly?'

She looked up to see Chiara watching her. 'Sorry?'

'I just asked where you're from. That's not an American accent.'

'No, I'm Australian. I'm from the east coast, north of Sydney.' Maybe one day she'd even be able to remember her home town.

'Have you known Pietro long?'

'A few months. But this is my first time in Rome.'

'So you knew each other in Tuscany.' Chiara paused. 'And do you—?'

'It's been a long day, Chiara. We want to relax, not answer a lot of questions.' Pietro's voice was firm.

Chiara wasn't in the least deflated. 'Then we'll make a time to meet when you're rested, Molly. I can show you some of the trendiest places. I'll call you if you give me your number.'

'You can reach her at my place,' Pietro said.

Molly watched as Chiara's eyes widened in aston-

ishment. For a second she looked almost disbeliev-
ing. Then she sank back in her seat, her eyes alight.

'That's wonderful. I'll call you, Molly. Okay? We
can go out together. I'd like that.'

'I'd like that too.' Molly enjoyed Chiara's bubbly
personality and the fact that beneath her teasing it was
obvious she cared for Pietro.

Besides, it would be nice to know another person.
So far she could count her acquaintances on the fingers of one hand.

'Excellent. I'll definitely call.' Chiara looked at her
watch and jumped to her feet. 'I have to go. I'm late.'

'It was nice meeting you.'

'And you, Molly. Very nice.'

With one last smile and a hug for her cousin, Chiara disappeared into the crowd promenading through
the square.

'She's very friendly,' Molly said, looking down at
her hand, still clasped in Pietro's on the table. The
sight sent pleasure tripping up her spine. No, that
wasn't right. The thrill had been there all along, like
a current of electricity buzzing on the edge of her
consciousness, but she'd tried to pretend it meant
nothing.

Nothing! It was proof, yet again, that she was anything but immune to the big man sitting so near. The
man who said they'd agreed to spend their lives together.

Her pulse quickened. The notion still caught her
off-guard, not with shock or dismay, but with the fer-
vour of her response.

Was it because she'd been so utterly adrift and
alone, waking in the hospital, that the idea of loving

and being loved by Pietro held such profound power over her?

Or was it because he really was the one for her?

Instinct shouted it was the latter. But could she trust it?

His thumb stroked the pulse point at her wrist till her blood beat faster. It took just that, such a simple caress, and she was putty in his hands. Yet she couldn't, didn't, want to break away.

Perhaps she should be annoyed that he was so obviously staking his claim on her. But Pietro's touch felt like support and encouragement. It was only now, after Chiara had left, that Molly realised how tough it could have been, facing the other woman's curiosity while she had so few answers.

Molly yanked her mind away from the idea. She didn't like to think of herself as vulnerable.

'Chiara seemed surprised that I live with you.' Molly tried not to make it a question.

Pietro shrugged and sipped his wine. 'I don't have live-in lovers.'

Molly blinked. 'Never?'

'Not until you. I like my privacy too much.' His gaze bored into hers and Molly felt it as a scorching blaze running under her skin. 'Obviously she realised you're special.'

Special. Molly could handle that. Particularly when Pietro looked at her as if she were his ultimate fantasy. That heavy-lidded stare made her breath tremble and her body quake.

She'd tried to be sensible and take things slow. But today, seeing Pietro with his cousin, hearing his humour, feeling his protectiveness and his love for his family, the barriers she'd erected had crumbled.

The idea of being Pietro's lover, even his fiancée, was no longer daunting but intriguing. Exciting.

A shiver ripped through her. Not from trepidation this time, but desire. Pure, unadulterated desire.

CHAPTER EIGHT

PIETRO WAS CLOSE to breaking point. He'd meant to seduce Molly slowly, so she didn't feel rushed or cornered. He'd managed just five days since her release from hospital. Now he wondered how he'd find the patience he needed.

He wanted her to turn to him, as eager as she'd been in Tuscany. But, despite her response when they'd kissed, she needed time. He'd seen doubt creep in when she'd learned they weren't married.

Even now Molly didn't wear his ring. He couldn't be sure of her. *He had to step warily.*

His gut clenched as he wrapped his arm around her and guided her out of the restaurant and onto the pavement. It was torture of the most exquisite kind, holding her, yet keeping a leash on the primitive urge to touch her the way he craved.

To have her naked. Beneath him. Gasping out his name while he powered into her.

A shudder ripped through him as he forced his mind back to the street and to the limo waiting for them.

'Pietro, is everything okay? You seem tense.'

He flicked a glance down to her upturned face, not

letting himself dwell on those glossy lips, or the intriguingly slanted eyes that shone more blue than grey tonight, reflecting the colour of her dress.

She'd blossomed as her tension had eased. Medical checks earlier today had confirmed she and the baby were doing well. Tonight she'd been animated and alluring, far too sexy for comfort in a dress that revealed bare, toned arms and a shadowed cleavage.

All evening his need for her had intensified as his control incinerated.

'Everything's fine. I enjoyed our evening. Did you?' Easier to deflect the conversation back to her.

For a moment longer she surveyed him, clearly trying to read his mood. Then she smiled. 'It was marvellous! The food was fantastic, and what a lovely restaurant. I thought at first it might be a little too…'

'Too?'

She shrugged. 'I don't know. It was so fancy, so elegant. I thought I'd feel out of place, but the staff weren't superior at all. I had a brilliant time; thank you.'

Which only reinforced what he'd already learned. Unlike Elizabetta, Molly neither expected nor demanded the luxuries and attention wealth could buy. It galled him that, even for a moment, he'd believed them to be the same—gold-diggers out for his money.

'I'm glad you enjoyed it. It's a favourite of mine.' He didn't add that he was part-owner of the place, hence their table had been near a charming inner courtyard, far from the prying paparazzi.

Pietro helped Molly into the limo and slid in beside her, forcing himself to look away as her dress crept up, revealing a flash of slim, pale thigh.

His groin tightened. His throat closed and he felt he was choking. It went against nature to stifle his sexual urges when Molly had been such a passionate lover, and would be again. Pietro was used to curbing his impulses, but that was in the business world. When it came to sex…well…he was clearly too used to getting exactly what he wanted.

Out of the corner of her eye, Molly surveyed Pietro, wondering what was making her urbane, witty companion so uptight.

It wasn't the first time. It had happened last night too. They'd been on the rooftop terrace when Molly had said she needed to turn in. It had been a lie. She'd been too wired to sleep. Too awake and aware of *him*. But it was either head to her lonely bedroom or give in to the urge to touch Pietro, as she'd longed to do for days. As she'd dreamed of doing in those erotically charged dreams that might have been pure imagination but which felt so real Molly wondered if they were, in truth, snippets of memory.

She'd actually crossed the space between their seats, not quite sure what she intended, when he'd stiffened and shot to his feet, stalking to the balustrade on the edge of the terrace. He'd bid her a curt good night, totally at odds with his usual charming manner.

Now it was happening again. At the restaurant he'd been great company, amusing and attentive, just as he'd been when they'd gone sightseeing. But now…

She shifted restlessly and saw him glance at the flare of her skirt across the seat then back towards the window. In the haphazard illumination from the streetlights his jaw was clamped, the hand on his thigh a tight fist. Tension radiated off him in staccato hammer-beats. Her pulse grew jerky in response.

'Thank you for a lovely night.' Her voice was husky.

What had gone wrong? Was it something she'd done?

'It was my pleasure, Molly.' He turned and smiled. But even in the dim light she realised the expression didn't reach his eyes. As for his voice, it was stilted, like their conversation. Then he leaned forward to say something to the driver and the car surged forward.

Molly's earlier ebullient mood frayed. Each day she'd relaxed more, felt almost *normal*. She'd found a growing confidence, despite her secret fear that her memory was doomed never to return. She and the baby were healthy and Pietro's enthusiasm about the child proved he was excited about becoming a father.

That insight had eradicated the last of her wariness. True, she couldn't remember their relationship, but it was clear they'd been lovers. She still craved him. And Pietro was everything she could wish for.

Except at times like this.

Had something gone wrong with their relationship?

Despite the kiss they'd shared, was it possible the physical attraction was only one-sided? Molly frowned. That couldn't be right. Pietro had been as needy as she had when they'd kissed. *Hadn't he?*

She had to find out. To bridge the chasm widening between them.

Molly refused to live on tenterhooks. If she and Pietro were to have a future, she needed to know where she stood.

She waited till they were in their apartment. Molly

was grateful the housekeeper didn't live in. She wanted absolute privacy for this discussion.

'We have to talk.' Her voice was over-loud in the lengthening silence.

Pietro's brow furrowed and he half-turned towards her, seemingly unwilling to look her in the eye. 'Of course. But tomorrow, yes? There's some work I need to do tonight.'

For a second Molly hesitated, aware that he'd neglected so much in order to look after her. Maybe she *should* wait till the morning…

Except she knew it was cowardice, thinking that way. Because she was scared what she might discover when she confronted Pietro.

'This won't take long.'

Molly crossed her arms to hide the fact her hands were trembling and strode past him into the sitting room. Its pristine, pared back elegance mocked her pretensions, as if asking, *Who do you think you are demanding anything here?* Despite its beauty, she'd never felt at home in this showpiece room. As if she were an imposter who didn't belong.

The trembling in her hands became a shiver that ran the length of her body, weakening her knees.

She whirled around, surprised to find Pietro close behind her. His brow was corrugated, this time with worry.

Unfairly, the sight made her impatient. She was tired of feeling like she was ill.

'What's the matter, Molly? You look flushed.'

'I'm confused.'

His gaze bored into hers, the flecks of golden bronze flaring brighter. He breathed deep and shoved his hands into his pockets. The action parted his jacket, making her aware of the breadth of his chest and the power in his long limbs.

'Go on.' He didn't smile or try to close the space between them. For a second Molly's courage faltered, but she refused to back down. She had to know.

'What's wrong between us?'

Pietro's eyes widened and for an instant she saw something like horror and a sharp stab of fear reflected back at her from those leonine eyes.

Shock made the air snag in her throat.

Molly was still trying to process what she'd seen when it disappeared. All she saw now was curiosity and confusion. And a hint of that never-ending store of patience that seemed to be Pietro's specialty.

Had she imagined that blank moment of alarm?

'What do you mean, wrong?' His voice rasped.

Molly swallowed hard but forged ahead. 'You're understanding and supportive. You're sexy and strong, and it feels like we're connected. And then, suddenly and completely, you withdraw from me, like you did tonight outside the restaurant. As if you don't want anything to do with me. As if you'd rather be somewhere else.'

Molly hated the betraying hint of a wobble on that last word. She dragged in a quick breath, and then another, aware that her heart beat too fast and her breaths came in choppy gasps.

Aware that she'd all but told him she wanted him.

Pietro's face froze in stark lines that accentuated the proud jut of his chin, that uncompromising nose and those narrowed, shrewd eyes.

Then, to her astonishment, his mouth split in a wide

grin and a shout of deep laughter reverberated around the room.

White teeth gleamed against olive skin and his eyes sparked with life.

'Is this your way of saying you *want* me?' Pietro's voice roughened to a sandpaper growl that scratched and teased the soft skin at her nape, her breasts and belly. And lower, down her inner thighs.

Stunned at her response, Molly stiffened, feeling abruptly vulnerable before a man who now seemed anything but diffident. There was something in his stare and the curve of his lips that made her feel like a small animal staring up at a prowling predator.

Pietro hadn't moved, hadn't even tugged his fists from his pockets, but he suddenly seemed much closer, his heat, his essence, wrapping around her, leashing her to him.

Molly blinked. It was absurd. She wasn't *frightened* of him. She *wanted* him. And yet she had the unnerving feeling that the careful balance of their relationship had shifted. That she was somehow poised on the brink of danger.

Pietro's expression changed, grew thoughtful. His smile remained, though now it had a sharp, hungry edge.

Slowly he pulled his hands from his pockets. It was a mundane gesture, the sort you saw every day without even noticing. But there was something *deliberate* about this movement. Molly focused on those big, beautifully shaped hands. The innate strength in them. The way they flexed, fingers spreading.

A phantom heat rippled through Molly and that scrape of arousal spread up to the apex of her thighs.

Her internal muscles tensed then softened in a telling signal of feminine readiness so blatant, it shocked her.

Molly swallowed as Pietro paced towards her. It wasn't that she was *scared*, she told herself again. But, though her body hummed with awareness, part of her brain was frantically trying to process physical and emotional signals that, however natural, now seemed devastatingly new and unfamiliar.

Face it, Molly. You can't remember sex, even if you've imagined it every night since you came to Pietro's house. As far as memory is concerned, you're a virgin.

'I just need to know what's going on.' Her voice was uneven. But, given the way she trembled, that was no surprise.

'What's going on is that I've had the devil's own time keeping my hands off you. Giving you space to feel comfortable with me.'

He stood before her now, so tall she had to angle her chin to hold his gaze.

'Really?' Relief made her wobbly knees even weaker. So there wasn't some horrible, dark secret? Was it simply that he found it hard to keep his distance too? 'Is that all?'

'All?' His mouth twisted into a grimace. 'Isn't that enough?' He shook his head, his eyes never leaving hers. 'You have no idea.'

His voice dropped to a low rush of liquid syllables she recognised as Italian. They curled from his tongue, running into each other, forming a velvet ribbon that danced around her, enticing, caressing and coaxing, delving low across her abdomen, drawing tight around her hips, teasing as it flicked her budding nipples.

She swayed a little, coaxed by the lyrical sound. Then he lifted his hand, cupped her chin and cheek with one big hand and Molly sank into his touch. Something inside her sighed in recognition and relief. Yet, even as it felt like home-coming, the connection ratcheted up the beat of her heart and the thrumming, insistent need that pulsed between her thighs.

Did it really take so little to turn her on? To make her tremble with anticipation?

The answer was a resounding yes. With Pietro it was that inevitable.

'I want you, Molly.' His voice didn't just waft to her ears but hit a low note that throbbed through her belly. 'I've missed you. I was scared I'd never find you again.'

Instinctively she pressed her fingers to his lips, stopping the words.

It hit her, a skewering thrust to her insides that, while she'd been busy bemoaning her memory loss, she'd spared little thought to the anguish Pietro must have endured.

She recognised it now in the raw, aching echo of his words.

'But you did find me.' She'd finally prised more detail from him—about how he and his staff had scoured the country round the clock for her, not just Rome, but the whole of Italy, and Australia too when the initial search had proved fruitless. Molly knew that even if he hadn't been rich enough to have staff help search for her, if he'd been one man alone, he'd never have given up looking. 'I'm not going anywhere.'

She dragged her fingers from his face and anchored

them around his broad shoulder, revelling in his sure strength.

His other hand closed on her waist, long fingers splaying towards her hip, the thumb reaching up her ribs. His touch was deliberate, perfect.

Molly shivered at the rush of sensation, the heady craving for more. She leaned into him till her breasts brushed his chest and the fierce heat of his body engulfed her.

'No, you're not. I'm never letting you go again, Molly. You're mine.'

It sounded like a vow. She felt it with every atom of her being and didn't doubt it for a second.

Emotion coiled in on itself, filling Molly to the brim. She'd wanted to belong, hadn't she? She'd wanted certainty. And here it was. Stronger, more overwhelming, than she'd thought possible. Briefly she wondered why she hadn't recognised and responded to it sooner.

'No,' she whispered, her gaze locking with his. 'Don't let me go.'

Deep down, Molly knew she could look after herself. That she was independent and capable, despite her amnesia. But to be loved like this. To be…vital to someone…and to feel that answering compulsion to wrap him close and keep him with her… Surely that was the most precious thing in the world?

'Love me, Pietro. Please.'

His response was instantaneous. A low growl of pleasure from the back of his throat drew every fine hair on her skin upright. The tightening of those hard hands against her made the blood sing in her veins. His tall body stiffened against hers.

'I held back because you clearly needed time.' The molten glow of his eyes mesmerised her. Or perhaps it was the deliberate quality of his voice. 'But now…'

It was as if a switch had been flicked on. From complete stasis, he surged into movement. One arm wrapped tight around her, hauling her up against him till her toes barely touched the floor. That unconscious demonstration of his superior strength made her feel flagrantly feminine. His other hand speared through her hair, dislodging the pins that secured it in the sophisticated style she'd tried for their dinner out. He cradled the back of her skull as his mouth slammed into hers.

The passion of Pietro's kiss stunned her. Sheet lightning flashed behind eyelids that had flickered shut. Surely thunder rolled nearby as he parted her willing lips and his tongue thrust hard and deep, making her shiver with delight.

His taste was addictive, like dark honey laced with whisky. Eagerly she lapped it up, fusing her lips with his, craving him in a way she'd never thought possible, even after that first kiss they'd shared. Each touch, each taste, each muted sound of pleasure made the need in her peak higher and higher. As if the days they'd spent together had primed her to a point of complete addiction.

Molly grabbed Pietro's shoulders with both hands, hanging on as he bowed her back over his arm and devoured her.

Eagerly she met his questing tongue with her own, angling her head to allow better access, digging her fingers into taut muscle in an ecstasy of need.

This wasn't just a kiss. It was a prelude to much more.

Her whole being burst into heated readiness for his, fire igniting and spreading to engulf her body.

Molly felt the solid weight of his erection against her belly and shifted, trying to climb his frame to ease the throb of yearning in her womb.

The hand at her back shifted down, grabbing her rump and hoisting her higher.

Molly's knees opened, spreading wide, as Pietro hauled her up to exactly the right place. Where the sensation of his arousal against the apex of her thighs was perfect. Or as perfect as possible while they were both fully dressed.

Had he read her mind?

Molly was aware of movement, of Pietro walking, but she didn't open her eyes.

Moments later the kiss broke and she felt soft cushions at her back, then Pietro's weight above her.

Molly's eyes flashed open. Above her was the shadowy ceiling of the sitting room and Pietro's face. He watched his hand skim her breast, closing on it and showering her with sparks of pleasure. She arched high, her breath a swift suck of astonishment at how right that felt. Even better, she realised, with Pietro's body hemming her in.

Yet her brow crinkled in a frown. They were lying on one of the long, cream sofas. And Molly knew, with a certainty that belied her loss of memory, that it wouldn't take much for her to combust. Already a running flame licked through her, intensifying where the bulge of Pietro's erection jutted against her core.

As if attuned to her thoughts, Pietro's eyes met hers. His mouth rucked up at one corner in a tight approximation of a smile. 'Sorry, *tesoro*. The bedroom is too far.'

There was a hand clap of shocked silence. As if she'd never entertained the idea of sex outside a bed.

Then Molly stopped thinking about everything except what Pietro was doing.

He levered himself up to kneel between her legs, his knees pushing hers further open. That small movement pulsed excitement through her. Or perhaps it was the touch of his hands on her bare legs, skimming the skirt of her dress higher and higher.

Air wafted across her thighs, hips and belly as he bunched the soft material round her waist.

Instead of fighting the urge to cover herself from his greedy gaze, Molly was aroused as his eyes heated and his movements grew urgent. She *liked* him stripping her bare, she discovered as he reached for her lace knickers.

Not *like*, she thought dazedly as there was a ripping sound and his knuckles scraped damp, swollen flesh. She *adored* it. Adored his ruthless single-mindedness as he tossed her ruined underwear aside.

Molly shuddered and cried out as he touched her there again, deliberately this time, his fingers slipping between slick folds and making her eyes roll back on a surge of eager pleasure.

'Pietro.' It was a hoarse gasp, a soft plea drowned by the thunder of her pulse in her ears.

Her eyes focused again as she felt his palm slide up to her belly. There was an extended moment of breathtaking stillness. Molly read jubilation in those golden eyes as they fixed on his hand, splayed possessively over the spot where their unborn child was cradled.

Pietro's eyes met hers. Something arced between them. Something so profound she had no word for it, no explanation, just an awareness that the bond between them was of the most primitive, unbreakable sort.

Then Pietro's hands went to his belt, tugging and flicking it undone, reefing open his trousers and pushing the dark fabric down.

A tiny part of her brain noted they were both still dressed—sort of. That she still wore her high-heeled shoes and they might rip the sofa material.

Then she saw his erection, naked and ready for her, and extraneous thought disintegrated. Her mouth dried, not in fear, but eagerness. She would have reached for him then, curious to touch, but there was no time.

Pietro came down onto her, his body covering hers, that proud erection nudging between her legs.

For a heartbeat he waited, his gaze searching hers. Then, with one slow, sure movement, Pietro thrust. Molly felt muscles stretch and widen, felt the impossible fiery heat of him invading her. But it was an invasion she craved. The silky power cleaving inexorably deeper and higher was beyond anything she knew.

She panted, unable to catch her breath. Stunned by the reality of them together.

Pietro's features, hovering above her, looked different, honed harder. His mouth drew back in a white grimace. His breath expelled in a rush of warm air from flared nostrils. Molly inhaled the scent of male skin, the tang of sweat and something else that made her insides clench and pulse. Arousal.

'Lift your knees.' That raw whisper didn't sound

like Pietro. But she'd seen his lips move. Now she felt his hand gently draw one of her knees up beside his hip. Instantly that stretched-too-far feeling eased. She wriggled her other knee up, pressed between Pietro and the back of the sofa. Now he sank even deeper. So deep, she felt him at the centre of her being.

Molly opened her mouth to say something, for the wonder and joy of it was too immense to keep in.

But then Pietro moved, holding her eyes as he withdrew, then thrust back hard and sure, and the breath shunted from her lungs in a rush of excitement. The pulse between her legs quickened. She pressed her heels down and pushed up against him, reinforcing the friction of his movement.

Molly grabbed his shoulders, fingers clamping through the fabric to the curve of muscle beneath. His flesh rippled beneath her touch, proof that the power of their joining wasn't all on his side. As if his taut features and laboured breath weren't proof enough.

Another withdrawal, another thrust that had her biting her lip to hold back a moan. It felt so good, so impossibly perfect.

Again Pietro withdrew just enough to plunge back with an erotic force that sent shock waves through her. The edge of her vision blurred. Something was happening to her, skin growing tight and tingling, and where they joined…

This time when Pietro pulled back he slid his hand between them, his thumb to that sensitive bud, pressing a caress there as he surged back to fill her.

Molly caught the glitter of triumph in his bright eyes as she exploded in a wash of gold stars. They wheeled and glittered through her body and across her vision. She arched, straining against him, as he prolonged that moment of ecstasy till nothing existed but the sheer rapture of them together.

On and on it went, till Pietro's body jerked in climax too, a pulsing, powerful judder that brought her again to that peak.

Molly was bombarded by sweet sensation. By the detonations of rapture still quaking through her febrile body. But beyond that was the sight of Pietro, strong neck arched back, teeth bared, shuddering with the force of an orgasm that she felt at the centre of her being.

Dimly, through the haze of pleasure, Molly felt her heart squeeze at the sight of him in the throes of the same compulsion.

For the first time since she'd woken in hospital they were equal.

Molly didn't understand quite why that was important. But there was a smile on her lips, and her heart felt full to overflowing. She pulled him down to her, palming the back of his head as he collapsed against her, his big body shivering with aftershocks.

CHAPTER NINE

HOURS LATER PIETRO woke in darkness, wondering what felt wrong. No, not wrong, but unfamiliar.

Even as he registered the sensation the answer came to him.

Molly. Sprawled across the bed and him. Her silky hair tickled his chest. Her breaths were tiny puffs of air that shouldn't have been arousing yet somehow were. Or maybe it was because her limp hand rested so close to his groin.

Arousal was inevitable. He'd woken hard.

Hell, he'd woken hard ever since Molly had moved from the hospital into his apartment.

Languidly, deliberately eschewing the urgency burning in his bloodstream, he stroked her hair, then swept his hand down her shoulder to her hip. She arched like a cat, pressing her breasts into him, and mumbled in her sleep.

Pietro smiled. He could get used to this.

He hadn't slept with any woman since Elizabetta. And that included Molly. Oh, he'd shared his bed for sex, but no lover was ever invited to spend the whole night.

His ex-wife's duplicity cast a long shadow. He en-

joyed sex but there was no way, before this, that he'd
give any woman cause to believe he wanted more from
her. He refused to tangle emotions with carnal pleasure.

That was what had gone wrong with Elizabetta.
He'd let other emotions get mixed up with satisfaction at her robust passion. Enough that he'd taken her
at face value. Or, no, if he was honest that had come
when she'd told him she was pregnant. He recalled her
charming enthusiasm tinged with uncertainty. His excitement. He hadn't planned children with her but it
was exactly what he wanted—a family of his own to
care for and cherish. To grow old with.

To give meaning to his life.

Despite his aunt and uncle, who'd done their best
for him when he'd been orphaned, Pietro had never
stopped missing the family who'd been wrested from
him. His mother with her wide smile and gentle touch.
His father who'd always made time for him, despite
the demands of the family business. Even his younger
sister, who'd been a pest in the early years, but who'd
begun to turn into someone he liked.

His aunt and uncle had struggled with a boy who'd
abruptly changed from outgoing and well-behaved into
surly and destructive. In the end they'd sent him away
to boarding school, hoping the staff would have better success with him.

Pietro stared up at the dark ceiling. They'd been
right. The regimen of school, and the kindness of a
couple of the teachers, had turned him around. But
that time away meant that, though he now had a good
relationship with his aunt and uncle, there was no real
intimacy between them. To his joy, he'd begun to de-

velop something like that with his two younger cousins now they were adults.

Molly shifted against him and his groin tightened.

He shouldn't wake her. She needed sleep, as she'd got little of it so far tonight.

Satisfaction stirred, an eddying heat in his belly. She was just as passionate as before. More so, if anything. As if any barrier that might once have existed between them had been torn away.

Because she believes you love her. She believes the romantic picture you painted. Lovers torn apart by circumstance and reunited. She looks on you as her saviour, combing the country for her, rescuing her from hospital, giving her safety, security, an identity. Love.

Pietro swallowed, ignoring the rasp, as if something sharp lined his throat.

The shards of his conscience?

No. Not that. Whatever a purist might say about his tactics, his intentions were good. Wasn't he giving Molly exactly what she wanted?

He'd seen the stars in her eyes, the fragile hope that last night in Tuscany, when she'd shared her news with him about the baby.

And finally Pietro understood why the sex tonight had been even more phenomenal than before.

Partly it was relief at having her back where she belonged. For he'd missed her. He *had* worried about her.

But the real difference was in Molly herself. Before tonight she'd held back something of herself. Of course she had. They'd indulged in an affair. There'd been no talk of love or the long term until she'd turned up that last evening with the bombshell that she was pregnant. She'd been guarding her heart.

But now...

Now Molly believed in him, in *them*, completely. Tonight she'd shared herself totally, with a generosity that had transformed spectacular sex into something almost transcendent.

For a while there he'd felt so close to her, so *at one*, he'd been both elated and terrified. She'd given him a window onto something he'd never known or expected.

Pietro's chest compressed as a weight crushed his lungs. It was the weight of Molly's expectations, her happiness, pressing down on him.

For a man used to running a corporate conglomerate that employed thousands, responsibility was nothing new. But this was different. It felt monumental. For a second something like terror crackled in his veins, till reason asserted itself.

Things couldn't be better. He had exactly what he wanted.

And so would Molly. She wanted him, wanted to be part of his life, wanted to bring up their child together.

He'd give her exactly that. *He'd make her happy.*

There was no reason for guilt. Despite the internal whisper that he'd taken advantage of her.

How could that be when he intended to deliver her dream to her?

The only possible problem would arise when, if, her memory returned.

But Pietro already had a strategy for that.

His mouth curved up in a smug smile.

Molly was a warm, passionate woman. He intended

to satisfy her fully, both sexually and emotionally, so that by the time she remembered the past she wouldn't be able to imagine life without him.

He'd explain why he'd overreacted to her news and she'd understand, because she was a reasonable woman and, despite her romantic leanings, a pragmatist. Otherwise she'd never have embarked on what had been originally a short-term affair. He'd assure her they had a future together, would become the family she wanted. She'd be happy and all would be well.

Pietro's hand flexed at her waist and she stirred again, her softness sliding provocatively against him.

Instantly his flesh tightened, his arousal strengthening. He should let her sleep. But, on the other hand, the sensuous way she moulded herself to him, even in slumber, revealed a sweetly carnal nature that matched his own.

Besides, if he was to bind her to him, shouldn't he take every opportunity that presented itself? Who knew when the mist of amnesia would lift and her memory would come back?

Pietro lifted his hand to her collarbone then traced the line of her body where she snuggled against him, down one cushioned breast and under, smiling as she sighed and rolled a little, unconsciously offering the pert nipple to his touch. Slowly he stroked a circle around her breast, feeling her tiny shivers as the caresses contracted in ever smaller circles. Her breath snagged. In the dim room he thought her eyelids flickered, but that was all.

He shifted sideways a little, rolling her off him and onto her back. Her mouth twitched in a moue of protest as if, even in sleep, she missed lying over him.

Surely, cementing her attraction, her attachment into something strong enough to withstand the truth of their situation, would be simple?

His hand skimmed lower, over lines of ribs, tickling the neat indent of her navel. The way she lay spread before him made it tempting to wake her with sex. He'd enjoy seeing the sleepy arousal in her eyes if she woke to find him inside her. But his scruples held him back. He might be in the process of seducing her into his life, but he understood the importance of consent.

Which meant waking her first.

His mouth kicked up in anticipation as he slid down beside Molly, tracing delicate, circuitous patterns across her velvety skin.

'That feels so good,' she whispered, lifting her hand to his shoulder.

Pietro smiled, hearing the catch in her voice. He pressed kisses at her hip as he moved to lie between her thighs. They shivered around him, clutching close as he swirled his tongue into her navel.

Her gasp was loud in the stillness. Pietro looked up to find her regarding him through slitted eyes. He smiled and lifted his head.

'Don't stop.' Her voice was sleep-rusty and infinitely sexy. If he'd been aroused before, the luxury of her body beneath him and the sweet taste of her made his need urgent.

Yet he refused to rush. He intended to be the romantic lover Molly expected. More, he *wanted* to take his time pleasing her. For there was magic there that made his own satisfaction even greater. Delayed gratification might be a form of torture but it was also its own, spectacular reward.

Propping his elbow on the bed beside her hip, Pietro let his fingers rake her belly, feeling her skin twitch and contract with the light caress.

There. Right before his eyes was the place where his baby nestled. Even now it was growing stronger by the hour. In a few months it would be big enough that he'd be able to see the swell of it. One day he'd be able to flatten his hand like this, right here, and feel it move.

His child. The beginning of his new family.

The wonder of this everyday miracle still astonished him. It made his hand unsteady as it rested on her warm flesh. He lowered his head, kissing her there, inhaling the unique scent of his lover—feminine musk and something light and sweet, like honeysuckle. It couldn't be soap or perfume, he realised. It was the same fragrance he'd detected when they'd been together in Tuscany. Whatever perfumes she'd used then were gone. This was essence of Molly. Pure, sweet and sexy.

'You're happy about the baby?'

Pietro looked up, over his hand splayed across her abdomen, to find her watching him intently.

'Never doubt it, Molly. It's wonderful news.' How simple it was when the truth coincided with what she wanted to hear.

And, Pietro assured himself, that was how it would be from now on. Molly's desires and his coalesced. Pleasing her would achieve his own goals. It was a win-win situation.

Her touch fluttered uncertainly on his shoulder, then delicate fingers caressed his cheek and jaw, scraping the rasp where soon he'd need to shave. Pietro turned his head, nipping at her fingers before sucking one into his mouth.

Beneath him she tensed, her thighs tightening their embrace of his torso.

Heat escalated as he felt her fine tremors. Pietro looked up to see her propped on one elbow, eyes fixed on him with an intensity that reinforced what her body told him.

Her luscious scent grew stronger.

Pietro drew her hand from his mouth and kissed her palm, using his tongue as well as his lips till he felt her shudder. Satisfied, he inched his way lower, aware of her shifting restlessly beneath him.

The triangle of dark-blonde hair protecting her sex was soft and tantalising, the flesh beneath already wet.

Pietro smiled as he slid his hand down, following the centre of her body to that tiny, responsive pearl.

She gasped when he put his mouth there, tracing her with his tongue, making her shake as he probed.

Her hands grabbed at his scalp then released as if she didn't know what to do with them. Pietro turned his head again, capturing her hand and stroking his tongue from the tip of her middle finger up the centre of her palm to her wrist, where her pulse beat so fast it seemed to quiver.

Satisfaction roared through him. Molly was so attuned to him, so eager.

He turned back, licking again, so she squirmed and he had to use his weight to hold her still. Her breathing hitched on a sob of rapture and the sound made him tight with need. He wanted to be exactly where he was, driving her out of her mind. Yet he needed to be deep inside that lush femininity, bucking hard till the heavens opened and the world collapsed.

It was time. More than time, given the way his strained body shook. Tenderly he nipped at her, felt the runnel of shock course through her, then sucked hard.

Frantic fingers raked his scalp. Molly's cry of triumph pierced the night and she jolted beneath him.

Seconds later Pietro knelt above her, brushing her hair from her face, watching the dark tide of ecstasy cover her pale skin. Her gaze melded with his, her mouth opened as if she was about to speak, but no sound came. Just the clutch of her hands on his shoulders as he knelt between her thighs and filled her with one hard, sharp thrust.

Sleek, dark velvet. Honey and heat. A searing, pulsing welcome. Her orgasm reignited, her muscles clenching, feeding the urge for completion.

'Yes,' she whispered. 'Now.' Molly raised her legs, linking them over his waist, pulling him to her.

With the second thrust she was there, meeting him, even as she cried out and juddered against him.

Pietro had never known anything as exquisite as the feel of Molly losing herself. The sight and sound of her. He tried to pause, to prolong that moment on the brink, but it was impossible. With a raw shout he followed her, diving into the shimmering, coiling fire, losing all sense of anything but the rapture and Molly. Molly, who even at her peak clung onto him as if she'd never let him go.

Was it any wonder, he thought dazedly later, as he lay boneless on her limp frame, that the world now seemed to spin in a new orbit?

He sucked air into overworked lungs and tried to marshal his thoughts.

He enjoyed sex. Always had. It was a good sign for the future that he and Molly were so compatible.

Yet this didn't feel like compatibility. This felt like so much more.

Pietro caressed her earlobe. Molly shivered and flinched. Even that tiny touch was too much in her overwrought state. A second later, her limp hand settled on his bare back, as if in mute apology.

It took Pietro a moment to snag again his elusive train of thought about how good the sex was with Molly. Dangerously good. Better even than he remembered.

It was tempting to imbue it with some sort of higher meaning. But that was the thing about sex, wasn't it? When it was good, it was very, very good.

Pietro told himself what he'd shared with Molly had simply been just that. They'd been lovers for months, so their bodies were attuned. Plus there was the added euphoria of knowing she carried his child. Together they were building the family he'd waited for so long.

That was all. Nothing more.

Satisfied, Pietro wrapped his arms around Molly and rolled onto his back, pulling her close and lifting one leaden hand to smooth her hair. Everything was just as he wanted. Even better than he'd hoped. He was in total control.

CHAPTER TEN

A WEEK LATER Molly dropped her shopping bags on one of the white settees and drew out the cushion that had caught her eye at a fashionable boutique.

It was silly to be so excited about her find, she told herself repressively, but she couldn't prevent the little fillip of satisfaction as she positioned it against the scattering of celadon and sea-green cushions already there.

She stepped back, considering. The bronze fabric was just the right shade to contrast with the greens she'd bought last week. And together… She put her hands on her hips and slowly turned, surveying the elegant sitting room. Yes, the combination was just right. Appealing and inviting. Far warmer than the room's original cream-on-white, which had looked like something from an upmarket magazine but was far too formal to live in.

Her gaze drifted to the throw rug in green and autumn shades she'd found a few days ago, not at an upmarket boutique but at a market stall. Then to the vase filled with vibrant daisies over on a side table by the windows. That had been her first purchase. She'd fallen in love with its simple, sinuous shape and bronze-green colour.

Ridiculous how nervous she'd been about display-
ing it in this designer-perfect room. She'd even asked
Pietro's permission.

'Whatever you want. It's your home too.' His words
had warmed her every bit as much as his kisses as he'd
drawn her close and proceeded to ravish her with that
single-minded focus she found impossible to resist.

Molly sank onto one of the comfy lounges, grabbing another cushion from her shopping and cuddling
it close. Her heart pounded fast and her mouth curved
in a grin.

Despite her recalcitrant memory, she was happy.

Pietro was, quite simply, wonderful. Ardent. Strong
yet tender. Incredibly considerate but, beneath the urbane gloss, he was potently masculine, the embodi-
ment of sexy Italian *machismo*.

She felt *cherished*.

A flutter of delight rippled through her as she recalled their love-making that morning. What had
begun languorous and slow had become hard and urgent when she'd whispered in his ear what she wanted
to do with him. In the end he'd been late for the office, but his final, lingering caress told Molly he didn't
mind at all.

She sank back, feeling like a cat who'd lapped up a
bowl of cream. Distracted, she surveyed the changes
she'd made to the décor. The room definitely felt more
comfortable. A place to relax. More like *home*.

That familiar pang of distress sliced through her,
but Molly forced it away, not letting herself panic
about her slow progress in remembering.

Her brain refused to yield more than tiny snatches
of the past, and never anything important. Children's

faces in the classroom. A long, sandy beach with the scent of the sea heady on a warm breeze. Riding a pushbike down a hill, the wind in her face as she tried to catch up to another girl about twelve or thirteen, just a little way ahead. *Her sister? A friend?* Picking mulberries and emerging from the tree with twigs in her hair and hands black with juice and the sweet, tart tang of fruit in her mouth.

Molly breathed deep and made herself look on the bright side. So far the little she remembered pointed to a happy life, a job she loved and a carefree childhood. That had to be enough for now. Besides—she slid a hand over her taut though still-flat abdomen—she and Pietro were making their own memories now, weren't they?

'Oh, you're home, *signora*. I didn't hear you come in.' The housekeeper stood in the doorway.

'Hi, Marta. I just arrived. I've been admiring my purchases.' Molly gestured to the cushions. 'I hope Pietro likes them.'

Marta beamed. 'He'd approve of anything you bought, *signora*. I've never seen him so—' She broke off and shook her head. Molly sat straighter, curiosity piqued, but before she could frame a question Marta went on. 'I like what you're doing with the room. It's warmer now, more hospitable.'

Molly's eyes rounded. She knew how devoted Marta was to Pietro. The housekeeper had never once intimated anything like disapproval for the way the apartment was furnished.

'I'm glad you think so too.' Marta's approval made her feel good. Even knowing Pietro was happy for her to use the money in the account he'd given her, she felt odd about spending it. And about changing what had been *his* home. So far the only things she'd bought had been for the apartment, not herself.

She stared down at the ring she'd put on this morning for the first time, the red-and-green fire incandescent in the opal's deep-blue depths. Warmth filled her.

After weeks torn between doubt and delight Molly had decided today to get on with her life. She couldn't remain in limbo, afraid to commit herself because her memory was slow returning. What if it never came back? She forced down a shudder of fear at the idea.

Instead she'd made the decision to trust her instincts and her feelings for Pietro. When he came home...

'There was a delivery while you were out. Some luggage. I thought you might prefer to unpack it yourself.'

Molly froze. 'Luggage?' Her pulse took off in a rackety beat and her breath jammed in her ribs. Pietro had assured her the search was still on to locate where she'd stayed in Rome and recover her belongings. Things that, surely, would peel back the fog blanketing her past?

Marta nodded, her expression sympathetic. She knew about Molly's accident and her faulty memory. 'One of Signor Agosti's staff just found it and brought it straight over. I put it in your room.' She paused. 'Shall I make tea for you while you look?'

Molly was already on her feet. 'Thank you. That would be nice.'

Minutes later she was standing before a navy suitcase on the wide padded bench seat at the end of the bed. Her throat was dry and her heart beat high against her ribs. She flexed her hands. They were clammy.

The suitcase was soft-sided and nondescript. She frowned. It wasn't familiar. Then she took a step closer and saw the bright-orange ribbon tied around the handle and her stomach dropped in free fall.

Molly's hand shook as she reached out and stroked the fabric. She'd put it there so her case would be recognisable on the airport luggage carousel. Her sister Jillian had laughed and suggested she invest in a bright-orange backpack instead. That had been what she was doing for her trip.

Molly blinked and found herself sitting beside the case, stunned by the vivid memory of Jill. It was the first true memory she'd had of her! The enormity of the breakthrough made her wobbly with excitement.

She pressed the heel of her hand to her sternum, trying to keep her heart from bashing too hard against her ribs.

Was this suitcase the key to her missing memories?

She reached out and tugged at the zip.

Half an hour later Molly was sitting in the same spot. The tea Marta had brought was on a nearby table, growing cold.

Molly's burst of excitement had petered out, grown cold too as disappointment and a strange sense of dislocation had set in.

She'd expected the discovery of her luggage would be a breakthrough, helping her recover the past, but there'd been nothing more than that first flash.

Dully, she looked down at the lace-trimmed camisole top in her hands. It was the one she'd worn in the photo Pietro had of her on his phone. But it evoked no memories.

There'd been a sense of familiarity as she'd handled the clothes and toiletries in the case. There was no doubt these were her clothes. The slightly scuffed ballet flats, the uncrushable skirts, the worn soft denim of the jeans.

But there were no flashes of insight. Nor was there a phone or notebook, or anything to help her fill the gaps. Presumably those had been in the shoulder bag dragged off her in the accident.

Her hands fell to her lap as she stared blindly across the room towards the dressing room.

Molly realised the discovery of her luggage had only achieved one thing. It proved that, whoever Molly Armstrong was, she was a stranger to this opulent world. One single top or skirt hanging in that elegant dressing room would cost far more than she'd spent on this suitcase and all its contents together.

She'd known she and Pietro came from different spheres but the stark gulf between them seemed more important with each item she unpacked.

Her brow knitted. Strange that she hadn't packed even one luxury item when she'd left Tuscany for her Rome visit. Pietro was a generous man. As his fiancée, living in his villa, she must have lovely things he'd given her, for he always seemed ready to buy her gifts. She'd given up admiring clothes in shop windows lately in case he ordered them for her.

Not that there was anything wrong with the clothes in the suitcase. They were just from another world. As she was.

Molly thought of her excitement at the changes

she'd made in the sitting room. As if cushions and a cotton throw could transform something designed to be ultra-glamorous. Had she really thought daisies in a pretty vase would make it somewhere *she'd* feel at home?

She huffed out a miserable laugh. Pietro's world was on a different plane. He, and now she, even had a discreet security detail when they went out in the city. The first few days, she'd been so distracted she hadn't noticed the men in dark suits who kept their distance but maintained a watchful eye on anyone getting too close. Now they were part of everyday life. Like the limo and the effusive welcome that greeted Pietro wherever they went.

Her fingers clutched at the fabric. All her luggage had proved was that she was an outsider here. Despite her hopes, she was no nearer recovering her past. No matter how strong her determination to move forward and build a future, the past was a ghost hovering on the edge of her happiness, threatening...

What?

She didn't know. Yet a premonition of dread settled in her stomach, warning her that she couldn't truly enjoy the future till she knew her past.

'Molly?' Pietro strode into the bedroom but halted as he saw her, shoulders hunched and head bowed.

Something hit him in the solar plexus, smacking the breath out of his lungs.

She looked so alone. So frail.

So unlike the woman he knew that anxiety climbed up his windpipe, one icy finger at a time, stealing speech.

Was it the baby? Was it a complication from her head injury? Some terrible news?

His gut knotted in the second it took for the thoughts to stab into his brain.

Pietro crossed the room in an instant.

'Molly.' He sat beside her on the bench seat and turned to face her, capturing her cold hands in his.

At his touch a shiver passed through her and she lifted her head, blinking up at him. She looked so dazed, Pietro feared the worst.

'What is it? What's wrong?'

Her mouth crumpled and he felt something carve a chasm in his chest at the despair he read in her eyes, now the colour of winter rain.

Then she sat straighter and shook her head. 'Don't look like that. Everything's fine.'

'Clearly it's not.' He paused then pushed the words out. 'Was it news from the hospital? That last set of tests?'

'No! Nothing like that.'

The urgent clamp of fear around his ribcage eased and Pietro sucked in a deep breath. 'Then what? Something's wrong.'

He noticed the open suitcase beside her and his blood ran cold. His hands tightened around hers. Was this the moment he'd been dreading—the moment when she remembered what he'd done?

'Did something in the suitcase spark a memory?' His hoarse voice was as unfamiliar as a stranger's. Silently he cursed. He'd planned to be here when her luggage arrived. His staff had been over-zealous, delivering it the moment the private detective had recovered it from the small pension she'd checked into.

Pietro had been in a high-level meeting and hadn't heard till it was over.

Yet Molly didn't shrink from him. Instead she clung to his hands. He gathered her to him, his heart tapping out a staccato rhythm that barely slowed when she leaned closer.

'I'm sorry. I'm just being a sook.'

'A sook?' His English was good but this wasn't a word he knew.

'A wimp.' Yet even as she said it she was sitting straighter, blinking, as if to clear moisture from her eyes.

Pietro shook his head. 'Isn't a wimp a coward?' Before she could answer he ploughed on, barely noticing the anger humming in his veins. 'You're one of the bravest people I know, Molly.' He paused, willing her to lift her head and look at him. When she did, as he suspected, he saw that her eyes welled with unshed tears.

He cupped her face in his palms, tenderly rubbing his thumb over her cheek where a single track of tears had escaped. Something twisted in his chest as he felt the hot moisture.

'Tell me what's troubling you.'

Because watching her pain made him feel wrong inside.

'It's nothing really.' Her lips curved in a shadow of her usual bright smile. 'I just got my hopes up.' She gestured with one hand to the crumpled, lacy top on her lap and the open suitcase beside her. 'I saw the bag and had a moment of recollection so strong it rocked me. I remembered Jill, my sister; even heard her words.'

Molly's eyes shone with something more than tears. Excitement?

He felt his own spirits rise in sympathy despite his ambivalence at the thought of her memory returning.

'That's wonderful news,' he heard himself say.

She shrugged. 'It made me expect…more. But even though I took out everything, touched everything, there were no more memories.'

Despite her matter-of-fact tone he heard the whisper of misery, of stalled hope, and felt a hot swirl of guilt at his relief that she hadn't recalled their final, catastrophic argument.

'Of course you're disappointed. It's only natural.' For the first time he genuinely regretted that tracking down her sister was taking so long. He wished he had some concrete hope to hold out for Molly. He knew too well how it felt to be left alone.

'I just feel helpless. I want so badly to remember, but there's nothing I can do to force the memories. And living here…' She met his eyes, her own looking bruised. 'I feel like I'm playing at belonging. That it's not quite real.'

A chill coursed through Pietro, freezing his grasp on her hands and constricting his lungs to a scratchy, sawing rasp.

But, logic asserted, Molly had no idea how close she'd come to the truth.

'You've been stuck here too long.' Better to focus on the practical than unsettling feelings.

'Stuck here?' Molly shook her head. 'You've taken me out a lot. And today I went shopping.' For some reason the words made her brow pinch and she looked away.

'A few sightseeing trips.' And fewer lately, when he'd had to spend time in the office. But he had responsibilities to the company as well as to Molly. He'd already neglected important business that could be put off no longer. 'You're used to being busy, having a purpose.'

It was true. Molly was passionate and lively. Not just with a lover, but in general. She wasn't an observer but a participant.

'You're used to working. Even here in Italy you weren't on vacation. You looked after three little children every day.'

'Until you swept me off my feet.'

Pietro saw the flash of delight in her expression and steeled himself not to feel regret at his subterfuge. For, though he'd seduced Molly into his bed, he hadn't proposed and prised her away from her job as she thought. On the contrary, it had been the news that her employers were planning to leave due to a family emergency that had prompted Molly to tell him she was pregnant.

'I suppose you're right,' she said slowly. 'I don't know anyone here, except you and Marta. I do feel a bit cut off.'

That's your doing. Keeping her close till you're sure you have her where you want her.

He'd even fobbed off his cousin, Chiara, when she'd rung to arrange a coffee outing with Molly.

His train of thought splintered as he finally registered what he'd been too preoccupied to notice earlier: Molly's hand in his. Not just slim and cool but, for the first time since he'd known her, wearing a ring.

Pietro looked down and felt a powerful jolt of emotion.

'You're wearing my ring.'

He traced it with his thumb, the hard gemstones a contrast to her soft skin.

Her fingers returned his grasp. 'Yes.'

Pietro lifted his gaze to her face and what he saw there arrested his racing thoughts. Molly swallowed as she met his eyes. Her cheeks were flushed, her eyes bright, not with tears this time, but with excitement and something that might almost have been defiance. Her smile was endearingly hesitant, almost shy.

Like a woman who's just said yes to the man she loves.

Could it be?

'It seemed silly not to wear it, given how I feel about you.' She caught her lower lip in her mouth, as if nervous about admitting it, yet she continued, holding his eyes with hers. 'I do want to marry you, Pietro.'

Another reverberation juddered through him. Surprise, he assured himself, and satisfaction.

What else could it be?

Pietro lifted her hand to his lips and kissed her palm, noting her instantaneous shiver of response and feeling its echo in his belly.

'You've made me the happiest man in Italy, *tesoro.*'

It was true. He felt as though he could conquer the world. His bloodstream turned effervescent, the weight he'd carried so long lifted in an instant, leaving him gloriously buoyant. Hadn't he known this would turn out just as he'd hoped?

His fiancée, soon to be his wife. His child.

His family. His very own flesh and blood.

Pietro pulled her close. His hand went to her soft, thick hair, grasping the back of her skull as he bent and kissed her.

Sweetness filled him. The unique taste that was Molly's alone. Pietro deepened the kiss, plunging in to claim her with a raw, visceral hunger that told him this was utterly, unequivocally right.

Molly responded eagerly, her hands digging into his shoulders as if she never wanted to let him go.

Her need matched his. Pietro felt the fierce craving for more. The need to take all Molly had to give. His erection swelled, drawing his trousers tight. They both wanted…

No.

Slowly, almost not believing his actions, he pulled back, defying the blood-deep craving for her soft body. Only as he straightened did Pietro register how he'd pushed Molly down towards the bed. It had been totally instinctive. With Molly it always was. One look, one touch, and he wanted her, *needed* the incredible heights of intimacy they shared.

But not this time.

Pietro pulled her back to a sitting position, wondering at his ability to stop when everything in him urged him to take his fill. To bring them both to the stunning rapture their bodies craved.

Yet, to his surprise, Pietro felt an even stronger impulse.

To banish the pain he'd seen in Molly's face and in her words. He wanted to care for her. To make things right.

Sex would make things right, but only for a short time.

He wanted to do more.

He frowned down into her dazed eyes.

'Pietro?' She looked as bewildered as he felt.

'What's wrong?' Molly stared up into Pietro's brooding features and tried to work out what was going through his mind. He wore that impenetrable look that used to drive her crazy but which, recently, she'd seen less and less.

'Nothing's wrong.' He breathed deeply, as if grounding himself. 'Everything's right.'

Then he smiled and Molly felt the breath drift from her lungs. That rare, dazzling smile hit her with the force of a freight train. Warmth suffused her and her brain grew foggy.

'Then why did you pull back?'

'Is that a pout?' He stroked her bottom lip and electricity zapped straight to her breasts and lower. 'I stopped so we could talk.'

'Talk?' Molly knew she sounded totally befuddled. But when Pietro kissed her to within a hair's breadth of losing herself it was hard to focus on words. 'Don't you want to make love?'

The last week had revealed she and Pietro shared a sex life that could best be described as combustible. Their need for each other grew daily. Surely she hadn't misread the intention behind that kiss?

'There's nothing I'd like more.' This time Molly saw the heat in his eyes and heard a stretched tight quality in his voice that matched how she felt. 'But first we need to discuss what we can do to make things better for you.'

His palm cupped her chin, then slid down her neck, and Molly wanted to scream that his body against hers would make things a whole lot better. But she was curious.

'Such as?'

'Such as expanding your social circle. You're used to being with people, but since leaving the hospital you've been stuck just with me and Marta. That's probably partly why you felt so low.'

'I wouldn't call that *stuck*. I like spending time with you.' And not just naked in his arms. He enthralled her.

Pietro was a great tour guide, finding quirky and fascinating things to share in this great city, so it felt as if they'd explored a more intimate world than that plotted in any guide book. He was tolerant, funny and good company. She was fascinated that his passion for football and fast cars was matched by a love of history and great food. That he'd been a successful amateur boxer in his youth, and that the sound of his deep voice singing an Italian ballad in the shower could melt her insides as effectively as any caress.

'Molly? I said how about meeting my family as a first step? You seemed to like Chiara and she's eager to know you better.' He paused. 'You might feel less… adrift if you get to know more people. I should have done something about that before.'

Molly covered his hand with hers, moved by his concern. 'Don't blame yourself. You were trying to look after me.' Even if Pietro had been a little stifling in his concern that she must rest and not go out much alone.

She suspected he even blamed himself for her accident.

'I'd love to meet your family, Pietro. After all, they'll be mine too one day.'

That dazzling smile returned. 'Soon. Let's make it soon.'

Molly looked into that searing gaze and felt her knees go weak. She loved it when he looked at her that way, as if she meant everything to him. Because she knew for certain now that this was the man she'd spend the rest of her life with.

She loved Pietro with all her heart.

CHAPTER ELEVEN

'How are you holding up?' Chiara grinned and leaned against the balcony railing of her apartment. 'The party turned out bigger than I'd planned.' Behind her, through the glass door, the party hummed.

'Great. You've got lovely friends.' Even if Molly had initially felt awed by the number wearing couture fashion. Chiara's friends were an intriguing mix of students, artists and the extremely wealthy.

Molly had told herself they were only people and she was probably just unused to mixing since her accident. Then, with Pietro at her side, she'd struck up a conversation with an artist and his graceful, high-society girlfriend, who turned out to be a budding author. All night she'd met fascinating, friendly people.

These days it was easier to be confident. She basked in Pietro's love. Before they'd left the apartment tonight he'd eyed her slinky slate-blue dress and growled that he should never have agreed to this party; that they should stay at home instead. The desire in his eyes, and the way he'd stuck to her side till ten minutes ago, when a business acquaintance had cornered him, made her feel like a million dollars. That horrible fear that she didn't fit in his world, that there was something wrong, grew weaker every day.

'I'm glad you're enjoying yourself. I wasn't sure if that crowd would be a good idea after what you've been through.'

'The accident?' Molly shrugged. 'That was weeks ago. I'm not an invalid.' Even if her past was still a blank, black wall. A tremor ran through her at the thought but she ignored it. 'It's good to get out and meet people. Thank you so much for inviting us. And for your friendship, Chiara. It means a lot.'

She and Chiara had clicked from that first quiet dinner they'd shared with Pietro last week. A few days later the two women had met for coffee and cemented the budding friendship.

Chiara reached out and closed her hand around Molly's. 'It's absolutely my pleasure. You have no idea what a relief it is to see Pietro finally settling down with a nice woman. After Elizabetta I wondered if he ever would. He spent the last few years pretending to be a playboy, which just isn't him. At heart he's a family guy.'

Molly felt something shift inside, like a gear thrust out of place with a jarring crunch.

'Who's Elizabetta? An old girlfriend?' It shouldn't surprise her. Pietro was in his early thirties and he hadn't got that sensual knowledge of a woman's body and desires living like a monk.

Chiara's eyes widened in such patent surprise Molly felt a tingle shiver across her nape. A whisper of premonition.

'Pietro hasn't mentioned her?'

Molly shook her head.

Chiara cast a glance past Molly's shoulder towards the crowded apartment. 'Maybe it would be better to speak to Pietro about her.'

Which sounded like a cop out. That shiver across Molly's nape now felt like jabs from tiny needles.

'Is she a secret?'

'No…it's just…'

Molly folded her arms. 'Come on, Chiara. How would you feel in my position? You can't just mention her name then back off.'

Chiara twisted one chunky silver earring then nodded. 'You're right. Pietro probably hasn't mentioned her because she's history. He's well rid of her. I never did like her.'

'But who was she? A lover? A business partner?'

'No.' Chiara's mouth tightened. 'She was his wife.'

'You're very quiet. Maybe we should have left the party earlier.' As ever, Pietro was solicitous, observing her keenly as he ushered her into their penthouse apartment.

'I'm fine. I enjoyed myself.' Molly walked into the sitting room and stopped abruptly. She was too wired even to sit. All through the goodbyes and the drive home she'd been unable to relax, but had been determined to wait for the privacy of the apartment before raising the subject of Elizabetta.

Why hadn't he told her? He'd already begun talking about their wedding. Surely it was natural to mention he'd been married before?

Molly told herself there'd be a good reason Pietro hadn't talked to her about it, but that didn't banish the raw ache because he'd withheld something so important.

A pang of distress hollowed her stomach and she teetered on her high heels.

'You're tired.' A warm hand closed around her elbow. 'Come on, Molly. You and the baby both need rest.'

Pietro sounded so reasonable, so sure he knew how she felt, that suddenly Molly found herself on the brink of anger. It was stupid. He hadn't done anything wrong. This had to be pregnancy hormones playing havoc with her emotions. Yet...

Gently but deliberately she disengaged her arm and stepped away.

'Molly?' Pietro's brow corrugated with concern. She realised it was the first time she'd ever walked away from him. Usually she revelled in their intimacy. It wasn't just the wonderful sex. Pietro was tactile, often reaching for her hand, wrapping his arm around her waist or nuzzling her hair, and Molly loved those caresses.

He's just trying to look after you.

But for some reason now Pietro's attentiveness made her feel ever so slightly claustrophobic.

How could that be? He'd only have to smile at her, stroke a hand along her flesh, and she'd melt.

Because this is about more than sex.

'I'm not tired, Pietro. I need to talk with you.'

He didn't move, nor did his expression alter, yet she sensed a waiting stillness that projected a heavy tension in the air.

'About what?' He gestured to a nearby lounge chair, but Molly didn't sit.

'Elizabetta.' She waited, watching for some reaction, but saw nothing. It was that impenetrable look again, rare these days, but still effective in blocking attempts to read his thoughts. 'Why didn't you mention her to me?'

Pietro shrugged and spread his hands, palm up. 'She's long gone, and good riddance, that's why.'

Molly frowned. 'Surely I had the right to know you'd been married before?'

'Of course!' He stood straighter, as if she'd accused him of something dreadful. 'But does she make a difference to us? To our plans?'

Molly opened her mouth then snapped it shut. Baffled, she realised he'd somehow put her on the back foot. 'No.' Her feelings for Pietro were as strong as ever. She wanted a future with him, bringing up their child together.

She didn't even notice she'd skimmed her hand protectively across her abdomen till his gaze dropped to the gesture. Instantly she let her hand fall. Still he said nothing and Molly felt a weight settle around her shoulders, like a clammy cloak, chilly and uncomfortable. She spun on her foot and strode to the door that led onto the terrace. She needed air.

'She was nothing like you.'

Pietro's words stopped her on the threshold, her hand on the handle of the open sliding door.

'In what way?' Molly didn't turn. It was easier to focus on the lights threaded through the garden, turning it into a romantic retreat.

'She was pretty on the outside but ugly inside.' His voice came from nearer, just behind her. 'Whereas you're lovely inside and out.'

Molly blinked. Silly, how his words stole her breath.
But he did that to her regularly, didn't he? She cared
for him so deeply, he was so ingrained in her psyche,
her need for him transcended the gaps in her memory.

'And?'

'And Elizabetta never loved me.' His voice was so
close it burred the bare skin of her neck and shoulders,
making her shiver. 'Not like you do.'

Molly pressed a hand to the place where her heart
battered her ribs. Her feelings for Pietro had been obvious for weeks, as obvious as his for her. Yet they'd
never actually said the words out loud.

A tide of emotion swelled, cramming her lungs so
tightly she could barely breathe.

'You do, don't you, Molly?' His voice was calm
but with an urgent edge that spoke of... Could it be
anxiety?

'Yes, I do.' The words sounded loud in the thick
silence.

Warm air puffed across her hair as he exhaled. His
hand skimmed her arm, up over her shoulder and past
the narrow straps of her dress to settle in that sensitive hollow where shoulder and neck met. A delicious
shimmy of sensation radiated out from his touch, cork-
screwing down to her heart and her womb.

'I really am the luckiest man in the world to have
you.' His touch slid away, down to her belly, where he
splayed his hand in a proprietorial gesture that thrilled
her. He leaned down and kissed her neck, sending her
body into overdrive. That felt so good, of course she
craved more.

But she fought her way out of the sensual fog.
'You're distracting me. Tell me more about Elizabetta.'

Molly hated the sour tang on her tongue as she said the name. 'Did you love her?' She didn't care if that made her sound desperately needy. She had to know.

'No! I told you, she wasn't like you.'

Molly felt relief seep into her bones. 'Go on.'

'We had an affair. I was actually on the verge of ending it when she announced she was pregnant.'

The floor dropped away beneath Molly's feet, but Pietro was there, supporting her, holding her close.

'She had your *child*?' Molly knew how excited Pietro was about the baby she carried, yet he'd never mentioned already being a father. This didn't make sense. Whatever his disagreement with his ex-wife, he'd be a devoted father.

'No, she didn't.'

Molly swung round, staring up into stark features. Instinctively she reached for him, clutching his arms. 'I'm so sorry, Pietro.' She could barely bring herself to consider what it would be like, losing a child. Everything inside her rebelled at the idea.

He shook his head. 'You don't understand. She didn't lose the baby.' He drew a slow breath. 'She was never pregnant.'

Molly frowned, trying to make sense of what he said. 'She lied?'

His mouth pulled tight at one corner. 'I told you, she wasn't like you. She was beguiling and sexy and, it turned out, a conniving gold-digger.' He reached out and rubbed at Molly's forehead, as if to erase her frown. 'Elizabetta had her mind set on a life of luxury and decided I could provide it. She knew I wanted kids one day, even though we'd agreed on a short, no-strings affair. So she lied, told me she was pregnant and that she wanted to have the baby.'

He lifted his head, as if searching the night sky. 'I was stunned. We'd taken precautions, but at the same time I was thrilled that they appeared to have failed.' He looked down at Molly and this time there was no guard on his emotions. She read his feelings, raw and real.

'I told you I lost my parents when I was young. What I didn't tell you was that I lost my whole family on one day.'

Molly sucked in a shocked breath.

'My parents and little sister were skiing in the Alps when an avalanche hit. I was supposed to be there too but I'd persuaded them to let me spend the weekend with my best friend while he celebrated his birthday.'

'Oh, Pietro!' Molly's eyes widened and her stomach plummeted into nothingness. How unbelievably tragic!

She clung to him. A trauma like that could change a child's life. More than most she understood what it was to feel utterly alone in a scary, baffling world.

'It's all right, Molly. It was a long time ago.'

Despite his words, she sensed the dragging sense of loss deep within Pietro. Was that why he was so very protective? Because early grief had taught him happiness could be transient?

'I know what it is not to have anyone close, anyone special in your life who loves you with that unconditional bond.' His mouth pulled up in a tight smile. 'I always wanted to have children and a family of my own, so I was delighted, despite my surprise at Elizabetta's news. Somehow she'd worked out that family was my Achilles' heel.' His shoulders lifted in a self-deprecating shrug. 'As a businessman, I'm not usually gullible. But the thought that she carried my own flesh and blood...' He sighed. 'I should have known better, particularly when she said she didn't want to wait for a big wedding.'

Pain pierced Molly's chest. 'You shouldn't have to expect people are lying.' It was an aspect of Pietro's wealth that she hadn't considered. Were there many people who lied to get his cash? 'When did you discover the truth?'

'Too late.' He grimaced. 'She tried to pretend she'd had a miscarriage while I was away on business, but her story didn't add up. Then she tried to convince me she'd been mistaken about the pregnancy and afraid to disappoint me. That she expected to fall pregnant soon anyway. But after a while she barely even tried to keep up that fiction. She didn't want a baby at all, as it would interfere with her lavish lifestyle. Instead she concentrated on spending as much of my money as she could get her hands on.'

'I'm so sorry, Pietro.'

He looked down at her, his cloudy gaze focusing slowly, as if it took an effort to drag himself from the murky depths of the past.

'It's done. We parted, acrimoniously and at considerable cost, and I learned my lesson.' He lifted his hand to stroke Molly's cheek. 'You can see why I wasn't in a hurry to tell you about her. What you and I have is so different. I didn't want to sully that by talking about her. But you're right; I should have told you sooner.'

Molly heard the tenderness in his voice, felt it in his

touch and read the regret in his eyes. How could she be annoyed that he'd wanted to keep what they had separate from his tarnished first marriage?

'I understand,' she murmured, leaning in to kiss him. She cupped his jaw, watching crimson fire flash at the heart of her opal engagement ring.

What they shared was strong and real, and just as magical as that elusive spark.

'But in future, I want you to talk to me about things, not hide them because you think I need protection. I'm stronger than that.' She might have felt weak and disorientated straight out of hospital but Molly knew herself to be better now. 'I don't need to be sheltered. I need to be involved. Okay?'

Pietro's gaze bored into hers, his expression doubtful.

She loved his strength and, yes, his masculine urge to protect, but it could be stifling. Rather than roll her eyes at his macho Italian male attitude, Molly tried to make him understand. 'This is important, Pietro. I want us to take care of each other, but as equals. So, from now on, no more secrets. Yes?'

Eventually he inclined his head. 'As you wish.' He paused, as if choosing his words. 'From this moment, no secrets.'

He looked so grave, Molly's heart skipped a beat. Was this how it would feel when they stood before witnesses and pledged themselves to each other? Originally she'd thought Pietro's suggestion that they marry soon was a little rushed. That she needed more time to adjust to being Mrs Agosti. But, feeling the earthquake of love and longing as she met his intense stare, she didn't want to wait.

'Is there anything else?'

Molly shook her head, overcome by emotion.

'Good.' His mouth kicked up in a sexy smile as he bent and scooped her into his arms. Stunned, she grabbed at his shoulders. 'Then, I repeat, it's time for bed, *dolcissima* Molly.' He kissed her on the mouth, hard and slow, demonstrating his intentions with a deliberation that sent desire streaking through her. 'Any objections?'

'Not one.' Her voice was breathless with a longing she couldn't conceal.

'Excellent.' He turned and carried her to the bedroom. 'See, consultation and agreement already.'

The satisfaction in his tone and the wolfish quality of that feral smile made Molly laugh aloud. Pietro did enjoy getting his own way.

It was only the next day, lying drowsily in bed after Pietro had kissed her goodbye and left for the office, that Molly realised he hadn't said he loved her.

He'd spoken of her love for him. That was all.

The realisation slammed into her, making her still, everything inside her contracting, as if plunged into an icy sea.

Deliberately Molly dragged in a slow breath and forced herself to relax. Her nerves were shot after the stress of the amnesia. This prickling in her fingers and the sick swirl in her stomach was just an overreaction.

She rolled over and grabbed the pillow where Pietro had lain. Dragging it to her, she hugged it close, shutting her eyes and inhaling his scent.

That was better. Her pulse slowed to something like its normal beat and reason reasserted itself.

So Pietro hadn't said the words. Did it matter? Everything he'd done from the day in the hospital till this morning, when he'd made love to her with such passion and tenderness, proved his feelings for her. She couldn't ask for a more caring partner.

Besides, men were notoriously unwilling to say the 'L' word, weren't they?

Obviously he must have told her before, when they'd first talked of marriage. Though Molly couldn't remember the proposal, she knew she'd never have agreed to marry a man who didn't love her.

Hadn't Pietro told her more than once that she'd made him the happiest of men? Didn't he show his feelings in every caress and passionate glance? In how he looked out for her and reassured her when she was low? Being with an amnesiac fiancée must be hard but Pietro never complained.

And he was clearly ecstatic about being a father. Every time the baby was mentioned she saw his excitement. The other day, as they'd walked through a park, he'd been co-opted into an impromptu game of football and he'd had such a way with the kids.

He'll make a terrific father. A wonderful husband. And yet...

Molly screwed up her face, annoyed at her neediness. Of course he'd told her he loved her. It was just that she couldn't remember him saying the words. Without that memory, the need to hear it from his lips became essential.

On a surge of impatience Molly flung aside the pillow and sheet and swung her legs out of bed.

Really? She'd lost a lifetime of memories and all she worried about was hearing Pietro say *I love you*?

Yet, no matter how she tried to rationalise it, the need was there, strong and growing. She could ask him straight out, demand that he tell her. But that wouldn't be the same as him declaring it of his own volition. She needed something to prompt the declaration. Some thing, or some place.

Maybe the place they'd fallen in love.

Tuscany.

Of course—Tuscany, a romantic villa. With any luck the happiness they'd enjoyed there together might also help her beat the amnesia that kept her past from her.

Molly shot to her feet and strode to the bathroom, excitement fizzing like Prosecco in her veins. She had plans to make.

'You want to go away?' Pietro swirled his aperitif in his glass as he surveyed Molly in the early-evening light.

In a dress of amber silk that skimmed her curves and accentuated her hair's tawny highlights, she was stunning and sensual. He'd had to make a conscious effort to act like a civilised man and not sweep her straight off to bed when he'd found her on the terrace, ensconced on her favourite lounger. But it was clear she wanted to talk.

'Yes. To Tuscany.'

Pietro put down his glass as something streaked through him. Alarm? His nape tightened as if someone had walked over his grave.

Ridiculous! He loved his Tuscan home.

'Why there? There are places closer to Rome you'd adore.'

Molly angled her head. Had she guessed at his disquiet?

She shrugged, the movement spilling her hair around bare, slim shoulders. Instantly the tightening of his skin spread lower, rippling down his torso to his belly and groin.

One look was all it took for arousal to strike these days. Even her sweet honeysuckle scent made him hard. Pietro had never known anything like it.

Which made it imperative he secure her in marriage as soon as possible.

Now, with his engagement ring on her finger, and her talk of joining the family, he was on the threshold of achieving that.

'It's where we met. Where we fell in love.' Molly paused, a fleeting expression he couldn't decipher flitting across her face. 'And from what you say it's beautiful there.' She looked away, staring past him to the roofs of Rome. 'I love the city but a change would be nice. Besides—' she swung back '—you want an early wedding and I thought your villa might be a good venue. I don't want a huge celebration.'

'Nor do I.' Partly because he wanted the marriage as soon as possible, but also for Molly's sake. She had no friends to support her, other than Chiara. Pietro had a possible lead on locating Molly's sister, but his agents still hadn't found her. He refused to ask Molly to face a big wedding with hundreds of strangers plus the paparazzi pack. Something intimate would be much better.

The villa had an added bonus. It held no memories of Elizabetta. His ex-wife had hated the countryside, refusing even short visits there.

He nodded. 'You're right, the villa would make a perfect venue. Private. Secure. With accommodation for guests.' Pietro paused, his gaze inevitably tracking back to Molly's generous mouth and sparkling eyes. 'And, yes, you thought it very romantic.'

He'd never thought of the estate he'd inherited in those terms. But seeing it through Molly's eyes had given the place a new perspective. 'You loved the house and garden, and especially the old olive groves.'

'I did?' She leaned forward eagerly.

'Definitely. That's where you first seduced me, under an olive tree.'

Molly's cheeks tinged pink. '*I* seduced *you*? I find that hard to believe.'

Pietro shrugged, grinning as he remembered her eager responses. 'Perhaps it was a mutual seduction.'

He'd made the first advance but Molly hadn't held back. She'd driven him crazy for what seemed an age, charmingly unaware of how alluring she was, playing with her young charges, wearing a wet T-shirt, swimsuit and floppy hat.

'Possibly. But I suspect you took the lead in any seduction.' She grinned. 'Who knows? Maybe I'll remember when I see the place again.'

Maybe she would.

The idea gripped like a fist squeezing his gut. But Pietro ignored the sensation. He refused to keep her from the place because it might spark a memory. He wouldn't live on tenterhooks any more, afraid of what might happen when she recalled how they'd fought.

Surely, even if her memory came back, by now Molly understood that he'd look after her and her child and give her the life together that she'd wanted? After all, she'd admitted she loved him.

Heat blazed at the memory of those words. Her expression as she'd revealed her heart for the first time. He couldn't remember anything making him feel as fine and proud, not even dragging the faltering family business back from the brink of ruin.

The potency of her admission still rocked him. To be loved—wasn't that what he'd craved all these years? To be knitted to someone at the most visceral level?

He vowed silently that Molly would never regret their marriage.

For *her* sake he wanted her to regain her memory. He could only guess at the burden her injury caused her. He'd read the strain on her face sometimes when she wasn't aware of his regard. The melancholy she'd banished so thoroughly that often it seemed like he'd imagined it.

'Okay, then. I have some meetings to attend or reschedule, but by Friday I'll be free.' He'd ensure it. 'Tuscany it is.'

Molly's brilliant smile smothered any last wrinkle of doubt about taking her there and maybe evoking memories he least wanted to conjure. He'd face that if it happened. He'd always hated deception. In some ways it would be a relief if the truth came out.

Molly crossed the space between them. With a sinuous ease that sent his hormones into overdrive, she sank onto his lap, her arms locking around his neck and eyes dancing.

'Thanks, Pietro. I'm looking forward to seeing the place where I first seduced you.' She shimmied a little, settling more comfortably. 'Maybe I'll remember some useful techniques.'

Pietro suppressed a groan as fire rushed to his groin. His arms closed hard around her and he bent to kiss her throat, inhaling the sweet perfume of her skin. 'I don't think you've got anything to learn, *dolcissima*.'

She was perfect as she was.

CHAPTER TWELVE

'IT'S EVEN MORE gorgeous than I'd expected.' Molly turned from the view of undulating hills to survey Pietro as he drove around a swooping curve.

She admired the way he drove, strong hands relaxed on the wheel, controlling the power of the low-slung vehicle with a competence that made it look simpler than she knew it was. But it was Pietro's profile that drew her attention. Those proud features looked harder, the angles more pronounced, the mouth tighter as they travelled the last few kilometres to the estate.

What was bothering him? Some business worry he hadn't managed to leave behind?

'I'm glad. It's my favourite place.'

He glanced away from the road to smile at her, banishing instantly the idea that he was troubled.

She breathed deeply, trying to stifle the flurry of nerves tightening her stomach. She'd told herself not to expect too much from this trip. That her memory wouldn't magically return simply because she was in familiar surroundings, But it was hard not to expect *something*.

And to worry about what it would mean if the villa didn't spark recollections.

Would she be doomed never to recall her past?

A warm hand closed over hers. 'Don't worry. Whatever the future holds, we'll face it together.' It was as if Pietro had read her mind. 'Just relax.' He withdrew his hand and shifted down a gear. 'And here we are.'

Molly turned to see tall gates opening. Beyond, an avenue of trees flanked a drive that disappeared around a curve of narrow cypresses. As they slowed and entered, leaves stirred in the breeze from the rows of grape vines on either side.

'You have a vineyard?'

Pietro shrugged. 'A small one.'

Molly wound down her window, registering the scent of warm earth and vegetation and, as they drove further, some fragrant herbs. She inhaled and a thrill of recognition coursed through her. It smelled… familiar.

'It smells good, doesn't it?' Pietro's deep voice burred through her.

'Definitely.' The scent tantalised, stirring something she couldn't name, and Molly tried hard to ignore a spike of excitement. She would *not* expect anything. That way she wouldn't be disappointed if no memories came.

A large, two-storey stone building appeared on her side of the private road. It looked very old but exquisitely maintained, with bright shutters at the windows, and beyond it a glimpse of aqua from an in-ground pool.

'It's lovely. No wonder you like it here.'

But the car didn't stop. 'That's the old farmhouse. The one Chiara manages as a holiday rental. You stayed there with the Australian family.'

Molly twisted in her seat, searching the building for anything familiar, but there was nothing.

'Don't worry, Molly. We'll come back later and you can look around as much as you want. It might trigger more memories.' Again, Pietro might have read her thoughts.

She sank back, taking in the green-and-gold landscape and, as they rounded another bend, the stunning villa before them.

Molly had thought the converted farmhouse was big but it was nothing to Pietro's home. Glowing a sandy gold in the sunshine, it was grander than any villa she'd seen. Yet, with its warm terracotta roof tiles and green shutters bracketing its long windows, the three-storey building looked inviting rather than intimidating.

There were formal gardens with low box hedges, within which were gravel paths, citruses in huge terracotta tubs, lavender and shade trees. The combination of perfumes—citrus and cypress, lavender and sunshine—made her nostrils twitch. Again she felt an undercurrent that tickled at the edges of her memory, a feather-light caress that made her brain quicken.

Molly heard the music of falling water as the car pulled up and noticed an ornate, antique fountain in the centre of the garden on her side of the car. It wouldn't have looked out of place in a Roman *piazza*. Yet it was perfect in this setting. As if it had been there for centuries, made by some master sculptor.

'What's so funny?' Pietro undid his seat belt and turned, one arm resting on the steering wheel.

Molly hadn't realised she'd laughed. 'I am. I'd expected something quaint and rustic; my idea of a Tuscan villa is more like the farmhouse back there. Not this...*palazzo*. I keep forgetting about your wealth.'

Which was absurd, given the incredible engagement ring she wore and the cost of her designer clothes.

Pietro's hand captured her cheek. He turned her face till their eyes meshed and that crazy, jagged lightning bolt of heat zapped between them once more. 'That's not important. What's important is you and me.' His gaze dropped lower with a possessiveness that made her shiver. 'And our baby.'

'You're right.' But the grandeur of his country home made Molly wonder how she'd ever had the temerity to begin an affair with Pietro.

Then he smiled, that slow, sexy smile that made her stomach drop to her toes, and she had her answer. Awed by his wealth or not, how could she ever resist him?

He leaned in and brushed his lips across hers, banishing confusion and doubt. No matter what, she had one certainty. She and Pietro were *right* together.

When he drew back, Molly felt ready for anything.

'So, how long has it been in the family?'

Pietro lifted his shoulders in that characteristic shrug. 'A couple of hundred years. But it wasn't in good repair when I inherited. The family business was in the doldrums and money hadn't been spent on it. I renovated it.' His eyes searched hers. 'Do you like it?'

Molly laughed again, the sound this time a bubble of pure joy. 'You have to ask? It's gorgeous!'

She saw his watchful expression morph into a grin and realised he'd been waiting. Had he really wondered if she'd approve? Pietro was so confident, sometimes bordering on arrogant, that his occasional diffidence took her by surprise.

'Excellent. I want us to be happy here.' He unclicked her seat belt. 'Come on. Let me show you around.'

They were greeted at the door by the estate manager and his wife who looked after the house. Then they were ushered through the building to a shaded loggia. It had a breath-taking view over the turquoise pool to more gardens then down to slopes of silvery-green olive groves. The breeze stirred and Molly saw, entranced, the wind's patterns in the sea of leaves. In the distance, blue-tinged hills framed the view.

'I'm in love.' Molly breathed.

Pietro slid an arm round her waist and pulled her close, his heat warm against her side. 'When we marry we could live here, if you like. I can do much of my work from here and just go to the city for short stints.'

She looked up into those leonine eyes. His tone was light but his expression intent. Molly leaned into him and kissed his neck, loving the salty tang of his flesh.

'Just because I prefer it here?'

'I do too, Molly.' He paused. 'It would be a marvellous place to raise a family.' His gold-flecked eyes glowed with that satisfied look he got whenever he talked of their child. 'Would you like that?'

Molly tried to visualise herself living in Rome, maybe working at an English language school. But the idea of spending a few years at least, devoting herself to her small family, sounded like bliss. How many women got the chance to be at home full time when their child was young? And in such a stunning place.

'I think I would.'

'Excellent.' His mouth covered hers. Molly felt the ardour in his kiss and in the taut rigidity of his big frame. Yet, instead of taking the kiss further, Pietro pulled back.

'It's been a long journey. Have some refreshment then I'll take you on a tour.' He invited her to sit at a table laid with cool drinks and delicious-looking sliced meats, vegetables and olives.

As they ate and drank, Molly felt herself relax in this peaceful, bewitching place. Everything, from the perfumed air to the food and even the luxuriously appointed terrace, lulled her into a satisfied stupor.

'This would make a marvellous wedding venue.' She could see chairs out on the lawn. The stone archway that supported climbing roses draped in gauzy cloth. It was truly romantic.

But would she have anyone to invite? Would she remember her past life by the time they tied the knot? Or would she make her vows in front of strangers?

She surveyed the pristine pool where, apparently, she'd come daily with the children, where she'd met Pietro, yet the past stubbornly remained a blank.

Molly bit her cheek, trying to quell self-pity. Pietro was trying to find her sister. When that happened, surely Jill would be a door to her past?

'Are you ready for a tour or would you rather rest?' Pietro's expression was solicitous. But Molly was fine now, except for the small matter of a gap in her brain where the past used to be.

'No, I'd love to explore.'

Smiling, he took her hand and drew her to her feet. It was obvious how proud he was of the place. 'After my parents died their estate was held in trust for me and a manager appointed for the business.'

'Not your aunt or uncle?'

'They had no experience running a corporation of that size, and they had their hands full trying to handle me as well as their own family.' He spread one hand, palm up. 'Unfortunately the administrator made some bad decisions and the business grew less profitable. Upkeep of the property just didn't happen.'

'But it's wonderful now.' Obviously restoring it had been a labour of love.

The villa was even more impressive inside than out. No expense had been spared. But, unlike the Rome apartment, there was a sense of a handsome old building aging gracefully. Of quirks and comfort. There were massive carved-stone fireplaces, a profusion of antiques, but everywhere flowers and big windows and chairs that looked so comfortable you wanted to sit and linger. The breakfast room featured *trompe l'oeil* landscapes painted on the high walls and rounded ceilings, making it look as if the long table was in an outdoor bower complete with trailing ivy.

'It's magic,' she said, wondering how it would be to use this room every day.

Yet, as the tour proceeded, an ache started up behind Molly's eyes. It couldn't have been from the glare from the drive here. She'd worn her sunglasses in the car and when they'd sat outside.

'Molly? Are you okay?'

'Fine.' She turned from surveying a library that would be sheer bliss on a rainy day with a fire crackling under that ornate mantelpiece. But as she moved she felt light-headed. She grabbed Pietro's hand, needing his support.

Was it morning sickness? She'd fortunately been free of that and even now she didn't feel nauseous, just a little giddy.

Yet as they made their way hand-in-hand up the sweeping staircase Molly experienced a strange shuddering inside. It felt as if her lungs couldn't work properly, her breath choppy and quick, each intake of air not quite enough. Her knees began to tremble, making her cling harder to Pietro.

They reached the landing, turned towards the bedrooms and Molly stopped, rooted to the marble floor.

'I feel...'

She shook her head. She didn't know how to describe it—not quite a headache but more a tightness in her skull. And in her stomach was a swooping, churning sensation that felt like the prelude to nausea. Her skin tightened into goose flesh and she shivered, cold to the bone. Apart from the physical sensations there was something else—rising alarm. No, more than that. Dread.

Pietro's broad palm covered her forehead. 'You don't have a temperature but you're definitely clammy. And you're very pale.'

An instant later he scooped her into his arms.

'There's no need for that. I can walk.'

'Not a good idea when you look like a breeze will blow you over. Besides,' his voice dropped to that rugged gravel-and-velvet tone she loved, 'I enjoy having you here, exactly where I want you.'

He strode down the corridor, carrying her as if she weighed nothing.

Despite the barrage of strange sensations, Molly repressed a smile. Pietro really did love to hold her, and she adored the closeness, feeling she was precious to him.

But as they entered the master suite she began to tremble. Molly had an impression of a huge four-poster bed, of windows looking onto the garden, then suddenly, to her horror, she was battling extreme nausea.

'Bathroom,' she whispered, her voice strained almost to nothing.

Pietro moved like lightning. She found herself gently lowered to the floor. She braced herself, grasping the sink with shaking hands, Pietro behind her solid as a bulwark, his arms around her waist to support her.

Tremors wracked her from her head to her feet, and she tasted acid at the back of her throat as sickness swirled.

'It's okay,' she found herself whispering. 'It's just morning sickness.' Relief settled, despite her churning stomach and that spidery sensation of cold fingertips playing along her spine. It was good to have an explanation. 'You can leave me.'

For answer Pietro widened his stance, as if preparing to take all her weight.

Molly was torn between craving privacy and being thankful for his presence.

Yet as she stood, bowed over the sink, the roiling nausea began to fade. After a time the sharp tang on her tongue lessened.

'It's passing.' She looked up into the mirror, finding Pietro's face taut with concern. 'But I'll lie down for a bit.' She still shivered and that headache grew sharper instead of dulling.

Instead of letting her walk, Pietro lifted her in his arms again, crossed back into the bedroom and lowered her onto the bed. It felt like heaven, despite the needle points of pain in her skull.

Swiftly he removed her shoes and spread a light cover over her legs. The mattress dipped as he sat beside her, slowly brushing her hair back from her face.

'How do you feel?'

'The nausea's gone, but my head…' She bit her lip and shut her eyes. 'I think I'll rest for a bit.'

'Good idea. I'll call the doctor.'

'No!' Her eyes sprang open and her hand shot out to grab his forearm. 'It's just a headache. Probably the aftermath of the nausea.' What did she know? She'd never had morning sickness. But it sounded reasonable. 'I just need some rest.'

'Nevertheless—'

'Please, Pietro. No doctor. I've had my fill of them fussing around me. Sometimes I feel like I'll never be free of them.' She knew the hospital stay and subsequent medical checks had been necessary. But sometimes it felt as though she'd been a rare medical specimen put on show for any passing medic. 'Let me rest and if I'm no better then I'll see someone.'

Molly held his eyes till eventually he said, 'Very well. But if there's no improvement…'

'I know.' She nodded, and had to prevent a wince, as pain lanced her skull.

Pietro stood, staring down with a furrowed brow. Then he poured a glass of water, positioning it and the phone nearer the bed. 'It's a house phone. Just lift the receiver if you feel worse.'

'Thank you, Pietro. I will.' She reached for his hand

and squeezed it. 'Don't fret. Millions of women get morning sickness and survive.'

His long fingers squeezed back. 'But none of them are *my* woman.' Despite the pain, her heart fluttered at his words. How had she ever doubted his feelings for her? He mightn't have said, 'I love you,' but he made it clear in so many other ways.

Pietro finally released her, moving to close the curtains. Then he kissed her gently on the forehead, his hand stroking her cheek. 'Try and sleep, *carissima*.' There was such tenderness in his voice, it felt like a velvet stole wrapping around her.

'I will.'

Quietly he padded from the room. Molly heard the door snick and closed her eyes.

There's nothing to be worried about.

The headache and the nausea were clearly connected. It had to be some strange version of morning sickness. As for that feeling of dread... She let her gaze roam the dim outline of the bedroom, experiencing a weird sense of *déjà vu*.

The chill creeping along her spine intensified.

Pietro opened the door silently and stepped inside.

On the bed Molly's slender form seemed incredibly slight, despite the rounded swell of hip and shoulder.

She didn't move, apart from the slow, even breathing that indicated she slept.

Nevertheless Pietro padded closer. As far as he could tell she hadn't moved. Not wanting to wake her, he stopped at the edge of the bed behind her. She lay facing away from him, her legs bent, her glorious tawny hair, dull in the dim light, loose around her shoulders.

Pietro halted, his hammering heart slowing to a more normal beat as he took in her sleeping form. Whatever had been wrong—and it probably had been morning sickness—it seemed to have passed.

Absently Pietro rubbed the heel of his hand across his tight chest. When Molly had taken ill like that, it had hit him how much she meant to him. Not just as the mother of his unborn child but because she was Molly, the woman he cared for. The woman he wanted by his side.

He'd come so far from the night he'd ordered her off these very premises. He remembered the explosive fury, the mercurial heat engulfing him, as he'd realised, or at least believed, she'd betrayed him in exactly the same way Elizabetta had. That she'd slept with him for long-term gain, even going so far as to pretend a pregnancy in order to weasel her way into his life.

Now he knew Molly for what she was. Innocent and honest. She really did carry his child.

More, she was the one woman with whom Pietro wanted to share his life. He'd married Elizabetta because he felt it to be his duty and he'd hoped that they might, over time, be able to build a life together. That had been an exercise in futile optimism. How stupid he'd been, conned by her!

Knowing Molly—so genuine, so warm and giving, so strong—made him wonder how he'd ever fallen for Elizabetta's lies.

He stretched out a hand to touch Molly's hair where it spilled across the pillow. But he stopped without making contact. She needed sleep.

Yet it was difficult to draw back. Pietro wanted to get into bed with her, slip his arm around her and pull her close. To be there if she needed him. To reassure himself that she was okay.

Molly had accused him more than once of fussing as if she was an invalid, but since that first night home from the hospital he hadn't thought of her like that. He'd wondered about her memory, and been wary of stressing her, but he didn't think of Molly as weak.

On the contrary, Pietro thought of her as feisty. Which was why she'd scared him this afternoon. He'd held her to him and been struck by the size of her, so fine-boned. She was average height for a woman but small compared with his rangy height. Maybe her indomitable spirit made her seem bigger.

Pietro straightened, shoving his hands in his trouser pockets so he wouldn't be tempted to reach for her.

His chest felt over-full, strained and tight.

His gaze traced the dips and curves of Molly's delectable body and he felt the familiar unfurling of desire. But there was more too. A tenderness, a sensation that was new to a man unused to strong feelings for anyone. A man who hadn't cared so much for anyone since his family had been wiped out when he was ten.

Pietro looked at Molly's sleeping form and knew he'd avoided telling her the truth for too long. He wasn't comfortable with deception. He abhorred it in others. No wonder he'd felt so uncomfortable these past weeks.

He huffed out a breath, audible and resigned.

He'd reached the end of this game. Molly deserved better. She deserved the truth.

He'd told himself it didn't matter because his intentions were good. But he'd lied, to Molly and himself. Now the time for prevarication was over.

When Molly woke he'd tell her the truth. She had the right to know.

Molly heard the door close then the snick of the latch.

Instantly the even rhythm of her breathing tore apart and she snatched a ragged lungful of oxygen. Then another. Even then it didn't seem enough. She felt dizzy, starved of air, though common sense told her that wasn't true. Those long, even breaths while Pietro had stood beside the bed had done their job.

It had been the hardest thing, lying here, pretending to sleep, knowing he was within arm's reach. A day ago, even an hour, she'd have reached for him. Pietro's consuming passion and his tender concern had got her through the dark days when the trauma of amnesia had been worst.

Her mouth crumpled and her throat closed on a well of rancid emotion.

She'd learned to lean on him. To need him.

She forced out a shuddering breath and dragged in another, telling herself that if she lay still for a little longer she'd summon the strength she needed.

Dully her gaze fixed on the dim outline of the small table by the window. It was too dark to see the detail of the framed photo standing there but she knew what it was. A photo of Pietro at age ten, a cheeky grin on his face. Beside him was a little girl in a frilly dress who shared exactly the same grin. Behind them a handsome man bent his head towards the woman smiling down at the children, as if about to whisper something in her ear. Pietro and his family.

Molly knew about the photo because she'd seen it before. The night she'd come to tell Pietro she was pregnant.

Hot moisture tracked from her eyes, across her cheeks and nose, to slide onto the pillow. She didn't brush the tear away because it was followed by another, and another, in an unending stream.

Besides, she didn't have the energy. She was too busy fighting the sensation that she was breaking apart inside.

Molly had remembered.

CHAPTER THIRTEEN

EVENTUALLY, AS MOLLY lay huddled with her knees up to her chest, the tears ceased and fragments of memory slotted into a coherent whole. She was still fuzzy about some things, like the accident, but the rest was clear as crystal. Horribly so.

No wonder she'd started to shake, coming upstairs to this room where she'd shared Pietro's bed. And his shower. And the chair by the window where he'd planted her astride him, surging up as she rode him till she lost her mind and cried out in ecstasy.

No wonder she'd felt odd in the library, where they'd been naked together more times than she could count.

It must have been the cumulative effect, layer upon layer of memories nudging closer to the surface till finally the weight of them had broken through the guard she'd unconsciously placed around the past.

How she'd longed to remember. Now she had, she almost wished she hadn't.

Except if she hadn't Pietro would still have been able to lie about his feelings and make a mockery of hers.

The pain in her chest swelled and spilled beyond

the cavity of her ribs, flooding into her bloodstream till she felt that ache in her fingertips, her thighs, even her womb. Her jaw clenched as she forced herself to revisit the past.

Most of it was fine, except the dreadful year she'd lost her parents. But she still had Jill and they were close. Molly couldn't wait to see her sister again.

And Tuscany had been brilliant. Most of her memories of her stay were bathed in a golden glow, for she *had* been happy. Because of Pietro. Because, despite him having made it clear he only wanted an affair, she'd fallen head over heels for the handsome Italian. He'd been macho yet indescribably tender, fun, easygoing, stunningly sexy and hadn't even minded having three boisterous little boys on the premises.

Because he loved *kids*.

Not you. He made that clear the night you came to this room, full of hope that maybe he'd be as excited about the baby as you were.

Molly gasped as razor-sharp pain shafted through her middle. She curled into a tight ball, hand to her belly, riding the hurt that just went on and on.

Pietro hadn't been excited. She remembered his eyes rounding, the gold flecks almost obliterated by gathering darkness.

Then he'd spoken, his tone glacial, each word like a splinter of ice stabbing her. Then the cool scorn had disintegrated and fury had exploded. She'd barely believed him to be the same man who'd laughed and caressed her only an hour before. She'd cringed against the bed, stunned by Pietro's vitriol.

He'd kept a marked distance, as if being in the same room with her contaminated him.

That, as much as his outlandish accusations, had given her the strength to fight her enveloping shock and stagger away, declaring she never wanted to see him again.

Molly shivered and pulled the rug higher, though this bone-deep freeze couldn't be cured by an extra layer.

Her thoughts slid to Rome. She didn't believe he'd searched for her. No, somehow someone had recognised her and told him she was in hospital and was pregnant. For Pietro Agosti was a powerful man with contacts in all sorts of places.

He hadn't visited the hospital to apologise. He'd come for one reason only.

Her baby. He wanted her baby, even if it meant putting up with her.

Nausea welled and Molly jack-knifed to sit on the edge of the bed, swallowing bile down her burning throat.

From the very first she'd seen he was excited about the child. He'd never hidden that. It was only Pietro's feelings for her that she'd wondered about. With good reason.

Of course he'd never told her he loved her!

Molly shut her eyes and rode a giddying wave of sickness, one hand pressed to her middle, the other clawing the mattress for support.

So many things made sense now. Disjointed instances which, when viewed as a whole, created a totally new picture.

The first time in Rome that they'd made love, they hadn't made it to the bedroom because Pietro couldn't wait. He'd taken her on the lounge. Yet he'd had time, while she'd been lying there beneath him, to plant his hand on her belly in a gesture she'd seen as both reverent and jubilant. She'd believed it proof he was as blown away by the incredible miracle of new life as she was. Now the memory took on new significance. He'd been thrilled about the baby all right. And he'd been eager for sex. But she'd bet his hard-on hadn't been for her specifically. Any woman would have done. Or maybe any woman who happened to be pregnant with his seed.

Molly shoved a knuckle in her mouth to stifle a cry of pain. Heat glazed the back of her eyes again. This time they were tears of fury. Yet Molly wouldn't let them fall.

How often had Pietro talked about the baby, gently trailing his fingers over her abdomen as if enthralled by the life she carried?

He'd claimed to be her husband, she realised now, solely to get his hands on their child. And when she'd challenged him on that he'd created a fake engagement instead, taking advantage of her in the worst way, because he knew how Molly felt about him. He knew he could play her emotions against her to get his hands on their child.

He'd have done even more. He'd have married her, cementing his legal right to the baby, pretending that he cared for her.

No wonder he'd wanted a quick wedding. He must be frantic to get everything wrapped up before her memory returned. That explained why he spent so much time with her. Pietro wanted to be on hand if the worst happened and she remembered.

It must have been a bore for him but the regular

sex would have been an added bonus. Pietro had a strong sex drive.

Molly shuddered but forced herself to keep going. To work it out.

She remembered what he'd said about Elizabetta. It sounded as though the woman was more interested in money than people, yet it seemed her major crime was in never actually having given him that promised child.

In this very room he'd accused Molly of being exactly like her.

Molly shot to her feet, unable to stand the flow of reminiscence. This whole thing, the scene they'd played out in this room when Pietro had ripped her dreams away and trampled on them, and the cruel game he'd played in Rome, made her feel sullied.

She flung aside the rug and strode to the bathroom. It would take more than soap and hot water to cleanse herself. The stain ran too deep. But she'd start with scrubbing every inch of skin he'd touched.

Then she'd erase him from her life.

'We need to talk.'

Pietro looked up from his computer, a frown settling on his features. Molly stood in the doorway, wearing the dress she'd travelled in, but her hair was wet and pulled back in a severe style that left her face pale and bare. Pale enough that the cute freckles on her nose stood out. Her tension was palpable.

He shot to his feet. 'Should you be up?' He knew enough about women not to say she looked tired but she was definitely unwell. She looked drawn, her features pinched and lovely mouth tight. Her eyes looked almost febrile.

Did she have a fever? Pietro crossed the room, reaching out to her, and slammed to a halt as she stepped back.

'Molly? What is it?'

'Not here.' Her glance encompassed the study and she shivered. 'Outside.'

'You need to sit and—'

'What I *need* is to get out of this house.' She pivoted and marched away.

Pietro considered reaching out and stopping her, but he was happy to talk where she was comfortable.

He followed her past the formal gardens to the olive grove behind the villa. With every step his thoughts raced. Was she unwell? Was it the baby?

Or had she begun to remember?

His belly clenched. It had been a risk bringing her here but one he told himself he was ready for.

Even if she didn't remember, he'd vowed to tell her the truth as soon as possible.

She halted under a gnarled tree and turned to face him.

'Molly, there's something I need to tell you.'

He wanted to wrap his arms around her, for he knew what he had to say would be a blow. But, watching her tight posture, he held back.

'Is there, really? That's a coincidence, because there's something I need to tell you.' Her voice had a discordant quality, like a cracked crystal glass that no longer rang true.

'You need to know—'

'I'll go first. It will save time.' Her words shot out,

harsh and quick. Something swooped inside him, like a bird of prey nose-diving for earth, zeroing in on some hapless victim.

'I've remembered everything.' The bald words grated across his skin.

'That's marvellous.' He stepped closer, reaching out his hands for hers, but Molly jerked back from him.

Pietro's pulse faltered. He stopped, seeing the cynical cast of her lips and her raised eyebrows.

'I'm so relieved.' He paused, ignoring her censure. 'I didn't like to say it but I'd begun to wonder if you'd ever remember. It's been weeks.' And, while it had fed into his plans to cement himself in her life, he'd been worried for Molly's sake that the amnesia might be permanent.

'You really think I'll fall for that? You have a vested interest in me *not* remembering.'

Pietro had known this would be tough. But Molly was practical; she'd understand when he explained. Plus she loved him. That knowledge, like a glowing ember at the heart of him, reassured him that her anger would pass.

'You're talking about that last night here? Before you left for Rome?'

'What else?' Molly laughed, if you could call it that. He'd never heard her so bitter. The sound made him wretched because Pietro recognised her hurt and knew he'd caused it.

'I'd made up my mind to tell you about that when you woke. It was time—'

'It was *past time*!' Her voice rose to a shout and she blinked, pursing her mouth and stepping back to plant her palms on the trunk of the tree behind her. 'You *lied* to me.'

Pietro winced. Her words punched like a fist to the solar plexus. Molly's defiant misery beneath the waves of anger did that to him.

He'd thought himself prepared to face the consequences of his actions and put them right. He was perturbed to discover things weren't as simple as he'd thought.

This wasn't a business negotiation where decisions were based on impersonal parameters such as profit and risk.

Molly's fiery silver gaze spoke of disenchantment and pain. Pietro felt it like a stream of molten lead coursing through him, searing his vital organs.

Suddenly doubt cracked his certainty that he could make this right.

A frisson of fear slithered through him, frosting his bones.

'I came looking for you to apologise. I knew as soon as you left me the terrible mistake I'd made.'

Her hands left the support of the olive tree and jammed onto her hips, her attitude pure aggression. 'You mean calling me a conniving gold-digger? And what about a greedy—?'

'Yes!' To his horror Pietro realised he was shouting, trying to drown her words so he didn't have to listen to the replay of his vicious verbal attack. He was nauseated, remembering what he'd said in the heat of the moment. His whiplash tone that had made her flinch and stare at him with wounded eyes.

Like the way she looked now. Except this time the heat smouldering in her stare spoke of disgust.

That sinking in his belly hit a new low.

Pietro heaved in a breath that didn't manage to fill his lungs. 'I apologise. I was completely wrong. It was just that it was so exactly like what happened with Elizabetta. A no-strings affair, then there she was telling me she was pregnant despite us using contraception.'

He'd been stunned, unable to do more than act on instinct when it had seemed history was repeating itself with a vengeance. When the beautiful, sensual woman he'd let into his life had apparently tried the same trick—to manipulate him into marriage with news of a pregnancy.

He'd spent years paying for his youthful gullibility with Elizabetta. He'd vowed never to be sucked in again.

'If I'd been thinking straight I'd never have believed it of you. But I wasn't. I was *feeling* rather than thinking.'

He grimaced. His track record with Molly was all about impulse and emotion, wasn't it? Even his so-called plan to seduce her into marrying him hadn't been based on logic but a desperate need to keep her close. Because he couldn't bear to let her go.

Molly's tentative talk that night about their future had ignited a fury he'd kept banked for years, ever since Elizabetta. It had exploded in a volcanic surge, searing everything in its path.

Because he'd trusted Molly. More than he'd ever trusted Elizabetta, even in the beginning.

It was no excuse, but it explained why, in his shock, he'd lashed out.

But Molly wasn't listening. Her mouth thinned contemptuously.

'Spare me the act about you feeling anything for me. I was just a passing amusement. I was crazy to believe I could be more. As for the story about you scouring the country for me, I don't believe it.'

'It's true!' Pietro started forward. But the way she looked at his raised arm, like a venomous snake about to strike, stopped him.

His heart smashed against his ribs. This was all going wrong. Why couldn't he get through to her? When he'd pictured this scene in his mind, it had gone completely differently.

'Even if I could forgive you for that—' Molly's glare pinioned him '—I could never forgive you for lying to me ever since then. For using my own feelings against me...' She faltered, her throat working so convulsively Pietro felt choking heat block his windpipe.

'I'm sorry, Molly. It was wrong, I know.'

'Then why did you *do* it?' Her voice wobbled but the fire in her eyes told him her anger was as strong as ever.

'I told you. They wouldn't let me take you home unless we were related. I couldn't bear to leave you alone in the hospital.'

Surprise flashed across Molly's face and for an instant Pietro thought he might have made headway. But the dull disbelief in her eyes disabused him.

'It's true!' He heard the pleading note in his voice and didn't care. He had to make her understand. 'I know I did wrong. I've regretted it ever since, and I wanted to make it up to you, to look after you.'

'To make me fall in love with you, you mean, so you could get what you want.'

It was so close to his original thoughts that for a moment Pietro was lost for words.

When he'd planned her seduction in Rome, he'd been complacent, believing he was giving her exactly what she'd wanted. A permanent relationship—that was what she'd talked about in Tuscany.

But, when Molly said it, his scheme just seemed grubby and devious.

Pietro dragged his hand through his hair, scraping his fingers along his scalp as he fought an unfamiliar sensation that the world pressed down on him. That he'd pushed himself into a corner with no escape.

'I thought you wanted it too.' He stepped closer, determined to get through to her. 'Us together. Don't tell me you can't feel how right that is.'

It was there now, a palpable connection, so strong even the anxiety churning his gut couldn't mask it.

'I've never felt like this about anyone else, *tesoro*. Believe me.'

He saw something flicker in Molly's expression. Awareness? Love?

His heart raced. He could do this. He knew he could.

Pietro unfolded one clenched fist to reach for her but her words stopped him.

'That's the first thing you've said that I believe.'

He rocked on his heels, his head jerking back as if she'd punched him in the jaw. Pain radiated down his neck and torso, intensifying in the region of his heart.

'Molly! I lied once, in letting you believe we had a permanent relationship. But I'm not lying about this.'

Her lip curled in an expression of disdain that made his tattered conscience shrivel. 'But it was a lie you told every day. As for feeling something different for me, that's only because I'm pregnant.' She wrapped her arms around herself. 'All you care about is the baby. I know that.'

'No! It's not true.' Pietro grabbed her elbows, needing to forge some contact with her. She didn't pull away, just looked up at him with a profound sadness in her eyes that belied the aggressive tilt of her chin.

'I care for *you*, Molly. You must believe that. Haven't I shown you every day how much you mean to me?'

Horror stretched his vocal chords so his voice didn't sound like his own. Because it was true—he'd told himself when he'd manoeuvred her back into his world that he'd done it because of the baby. Now he realised he'd deluded himself, whether from pride or fear at the depth of his feelings for Molly.

'Of course I care for our baby, but it's *you*—'

'Don't! Just...don't.' She sucked in a shuddery breath and he felt her whole body tremble. 'I can't take any more, Pietro.' She paused, her brow furrowing. 'I can't even bear to have you touch me.'

Stunned, he read sincerity in Molly's stormy eyes. Immediately he let go, stumbling backwards and shoving his hands deep in his pockets.

Everything inside him collapsed in on itself.

Pain engulfed him.

All his certainties shattered. About Molly. About himself.

'You don't love me?'

He was too disorientated even to be embarrassed as the question slipped past his guard. He sounded like a lonely kid. Like that ten-year-old who'd found himself alone and unloved.

He sounded needy. Desperate.

He'd been about to declare his feelings for her but what magic would they work if Molly didn't love him back? Or even believe him.

He'd grown used to her love, he realised. He'd been relishing it. Using it as a basis to build dreams for the future.

Now everything he'd hoped for, everything he'd been sure of, disintegrated.

Molly's mouth crumpled as she blinked up at him, her eyes awash. The sight pierced his chest with remorse.

'You had to rub it in, didn't you? That I was so gullible.' She drew herself up and went on before he could find words she might listen to. 'Yes, I loved you.' The past tense was like a death knell. 'But now I think I hate you. I can't bear to look at you, Pietro. If you have any shred of decency or respect for me, you won't stand in my way.'

What could he do but give her space?

Yet even as she stumbled past him Pietro fought the impulse to catch her close, imprison her and persuade her with his hands, his body and his words that they were meant to be together. Not because of the baby they'd made but because she loved him and he loved her.

He loved her.

It was that which made him stand his ground as she hurried back to the villa, even though it went against every instinct. Because loving meant respecting her wishes.

He loved her.

It was so simple and at the same time so huge, so momentous.

He'd known for a long time that Molly was different. That his feelings for her transcended anything he'd felt for any other woman.

Pietro reached out a hand and leaned against the old olive tree, its bark rough against his palm, seemingly the only solid thing in a world turned on its head.

It was late when he returned to the villa, but the time spent considering his mistakes hadn't brought any solutions, just a feeling of dislocation.

When his housekeeper brought him a note from Molly he was surprised to discover he hadn't yet plumbed the depths of misery. That came when he read her words...

I'm going home to Australia. Don't follow me or try to stop me. I've had enough.

That was when Pietro discovered how Molly had felt. When his heart split apart.

CHAPTER FOURTEEN

PIETRO TURNED OFF the engine of the hire car. The motor ticked in the early-morning silence as he surveyed the house. He wasn't delaying, just scoping the environment, as he would prior to any major business negotiation.

Yet his heart beat hard against his ribs and adrenalin buzzed in his blood.

He pinched the bridge of his nose, forcing back a headache. His eyes were scratchy from lack of sleep. Logic said he should delay till he'd rested after the long trip to Australia, but waiting was impossible. Sleep had eluded him last night.

The other houses in the street were large, modern buildings that took up all the space on their plot. By contrast, number sixty-three was a throwback to an earlier generation. Single-storeyed, wooden and painted in a shade of pastel green with white trim, it was far smaller yet appealing. It sat in a garden of thick, cropped grass and slender trees with narrow leaves through which he saw the mirrored surface of the bay just beyond the house.

It looked…inviting.

Pietro's breath expelled in a harsh grunt that might have been a laugh but he feared was a groan.

Doubt assailed him. Not about the wisdom of what he was doing—about that he had no qualms; honour demanded he follow through. No, his doubt was about the outcome of this trip.

His hand clenched on the steering wheel as emotion slammed him. He'd done his best to keep himself busy on the long flight to Australia, to distract himself from feeling anything. But there were limits and he'd reached his. No matter what he did, no matter how logically he approached this, he couldn't ignore the profound well of despair that sucked him in deeper each day.

There was no way out. No way could he ever convince Molly of his true feelings. *That was his punishment.*

He closed burning eyes. Ironic, wasn't it, that he, the man who'd schemed to seduce her into falling in love, had been the one to fall in love?

He loved a woman who never wanted to see him again.

As if that wasn't bad enough, his monumental blindness mocked him. He'd prided himself on having pulled his faltering family business from the edge of ruin and turning it into a success story. He'd prided himself on his judgement. Yet he hadn't seen what was right in front of him.

He hadn't fallen in love in Rome while winning Molly over. He'd loved her before that, had fallen for her in Tuscany, but hadn't recognised the depth of his feelings. That was why, in the moment of insanity when he'd believed she'd used him, he'd snapped and let loose that string of damning accusations. Because the pain had been unbearable.

As it was now.

Pietro snapped his eyes open and stared at the neat little house in its bower of green.

Despite its charm the sight of it chilled him. The odds were that this was where any hope of the future he craved would finally shrivel and die.

Swiftly, before he changed his mind, he unclicked his seat belt and grabbed the envelope from the seat beside him. He got out of the car and a cold breeze hit his face, a reminder that it was winter on this side of the world.

Pietro swallowed, noting the sour tang on his tongue. Fear? Defeat? It didn't matter. He had to do this.

He crossed the silent street and, despite everything, felt excited at the prospect of seeing Molly again. Surely there was a chance he could convince her?

As he stepped onto the property she and her sister had inherited from their parents, a raucous sound made him start. He looked up into the trees and saw a bird with a powerful beak turned up towards the sky, its whole body shaking as it called. A kookaburra, laughing as if at some cosmic joke.

Molly swallowed the last mouthful of toast as she padded to the front door. There she paused, raking her hair from her face. She wore ancient jeans, thick socks and her shirt had seen better days but she hadn't expected visitors. With Jillian in Sydney for a job interview, Molly had a day alone.

A day to mope and feel sorry for herself.

Sighing, she pushed back her shoulders. If it was that estate agent again, trying to talk her into selling the house, he'd get short shrift.

She pulled open the door and froze. All except for her heart, which somersaulted, then knocked against her ribcage.

Her fingers on the doorknob tightened to the point of pain. A mighty shudder wracked her, making her glad she held onto something solid.

'Hello, Molly.'

His voice was the same, that rich honey and whisky voice that did unspeakably potent things to her willpower. She felt herself sag and was powerless to stop it.

She'd dreamed of this. Of Pietro coming after her. Despite the dictates of common sense, pride and all her resolve, it had been Molly's secret, guilty pleasure.

He even looked the same. Suave and urbane in his Italian suit, yet with an air of masculine power that even now made her knees tremble.

She lifted her chin, peering up into his face, but the slanting sun was behind him and she couldn't read his expression.

Memories bombarded her. Of the first time she'd seen him in a suit, when he'd watched her from the doorway of her hospital room. Of those wide shoulders, naked and gleaming with sweat, rising above her as they made love on a picnic blanket in that ancient grove. Of his expression as he admitted he'd lied to her, not once but for weeks, all to get his hands on their baby.

For the first time in weeks, nausea churned.

'What are you doing here?'

He stiffened, those impressive shoulders lifting as if drawn tight. Had he expected a welcome?

'I have news for you.' He paused. 'May I come in?'

Molly blinked up at him. She was torn between competing urges. To step back or shut the door in his face. For surely there was no news that would change anything? He'd lied to get his hands on her baby. That was unforgivable. And yet...

And yet she was so weak she found herself eating him up with her hungry gaze, canting forward, drawn by that familiar aftershave and, beneath it, that spicy, tantalisingly delicious scent she knew was simply Pietro.

She'd longed for him. Sometimes, in her lonely bed, she'd even pretended she'd read real distress on his face that last day.

Of course he'd been distressed. She'd finally seen through his plan to con her.

'I don't think that's a good idea.'

His head jerked back as if she'd slapped him and, despite herself, sympathy stirred.

When he spoke again his voice was stretched and hoarse, almost as if it hurt him to speak. 'I've come a long way to see you. I'd hoped to do this in person.'

He gestured with one hand and she realised he held a large envelope. Instantly her insides clenched in fear. What was it? The beginning of some legal wrangle over their baby?

Her free hand lifted, as if to slide protectively over her belly, but she curtailed the gesture, determined not to reveal any frailty in front of him. But that didn't prevent the horrible, jittery sensation of nerves.

'Very well.' She stepped aside and gestured him in. Better to hear the news from Pietro. If she sent him away she'd just worry herself stupid over what action he planned to take.

With his wealth and power he could outgun her in any legal manoeuvre. Her skin iced at the possibilities.

Pietro stepped over the threshold and instantly the air clogged in her windpipe. He took up all the space in the narrow hall. How had she forgotten how big he was? She had to sidle round him, ultra-conscious of his tall frame as she slipped past.

Molly had forgotten too, the sensation of Pietro's gaze on her, heavy as a hand stroking her back, as she led the way to the family room looking out over the water.

'Please, take a seat.' She didn't look at him but sank into her favourite armchair, grateful to sit, as her legs wouldn't hold her much longer.

'Thank you.'

Finally Molly made herself look directly at him.

She stifled a gasp, for the man staring back at her wasn't the man she remembered. Those high-cut cheekbones were painfully prominent, his face drawn, and around his mouth deep grooves had settled. Startled, she lifted her gaze to his eyes. They looked straight back, but instead of that golden glow she remembered his eyes seemed dimmed.

Molly bit her lip, disturbed by the change in him. 'You've just travelled from Italy?'

He nodded. 'I arrived in Sydney late last night.'

That explained it. He was probably jet-lagged. 'You

must have got up early.' Her family home was several hours' drive north of the city.

'I drove up last night.'

Molly's eyes rounded. 'But where did you stay?' Despite the recent real-estate boom, there were no five-star hotels in the vicinity.

He shrugged. 'There's a motel a few kilometres away.'

Motel? Molly stared, grappling with the fact her billionaire ex-lover had stayed in a cheap motel that generally attracted families and travelling salesmen.

She sank back, head reeling. Had he brought his security team too? Had they all spent the night at the down-at-heel Golden Sands Motel?

Was this a dream?

Pietro shifted in his seat and Molly heard the twang of springs on the ancient lounge chair. No, this was real. Pietro was in her home. On business so important it couldn't wait.

'You're going to fight for custody.' Despite the up-surge of fear, her voice was resigned. Hadn't she ex-pected this? She told herself it was almost a relief to have it out in the open. It had been weeks since she'd left Rome, and daily she'd wondered when Pi-etro would make a move to secure his child.

Pietro surged forward in his seat, the springs pro-testing the movement.

'No! Nothing like that.'

'Pardon?' Molly's fingers dug into the fabric of her own seat.

His jaw worked and she watched, fascinated by the hectic throb of a pulse at his temple. It struck her that, apart from the exquisitely crafted suit, Pietro didn't look like a powerful tycoon. He looked like a man on the edge. A man fighting the same tangle of raw emotions that enmeshed her.

But how likely was that?

She had to stop projecting her emotions onto him. That was the trap she'd fallen into in Italy. Firstly in Tuscany, believing he loved her as she had him, then in Rome, reading love into his possessive attitude when all he cared about was her baby, not her.

She swallowed, disappointment bitter on her tongue.

'I'm not here to take the child from you, Molly. I'd never do that.'

Molly's breath jammed. Could it be? Or was this some game?

Bewildered, she tried to marshal her thoughts. Despite the way he'd played her, she knew Pietro wasn't all bad. When Molly had arrived in Sydney, stressed and exhausted, she'd been dumbstruck to discover a chauffeur waiting at the airport with instructions to drive her wherever she wanted to go, courtesy of Pietro. And it had been Pietro who'd finally located her sister Jillian, informed her of Molly's accident and arranged for her immediate flight to Australia. She'd arrived just a day after Molly.

The man who'd done that couldn't be so cruel as to lie now about something as important as their child.

She squeezed her eyes shut, telling herself she was doing it again, reading what she wanted into the situation. It was guilt motivating him, or the need to look good if it came to a court case.

Her eyes snapped open and she saw Pietro leaning towards her, wearing a look of such pain that her chest squeezed.

As she watched, he sat back, his features settling into something approximating his old unreadable expression. Yet either Pietro wasn't quite as inscrutable as he used to be or Molly's ability to read him had improved. She saw tension and pain, plus something she couldn't name.

She opened her mouth but before she could speak Pietro leaned across, offering her the envelope.

'As you see, it's not about custody.' Even so, Molly's hands were clammy with fear as she took it and withdrew an official-looking document. 'I had it drawn up in English to make it easier for you.'

Drawing a deep breath, she stared down at the papers. Nevertheless, it took an age before she could focus. She was too aware of Pietro leaning close, intent on her. And of her heart beating a frantic tattoo against her ribs.

Finally, words began to penetrate. As they did, astonishment rose, swamping fear. She reread the paragraphs she'd only skimmed.

Pietro had told the truth. There was no mention of their baby. This was all about her.

'You're *giving* me your villa in Tuscany?' Not just the villa, but the whole estate, including several farm houses, as well as a productive vineyard and olive grove.

'*Si.*'

Molly kept reading, looking for a catch, for some clause stating that by accepting she would give Pietro rights over her child. But there was nothing. Just the simple statement that she was now the owner of the estate, plus a hefty sum of money.

'I don't understand.' She looked up, her eyes meeting his. A shot of adrenalin ripped through her, stealing her breath.

'I've made the estate over to you. It's my hope that you and our child will live there, at least part of the time.'

See? There was a catch. 'So you *do* want custody. Or at least to share it. That's why you want the baby raised in Italy.' Molly didn't know Italian law but guessed it might support a father taking control of his child's life.

'No!' Pietro jerked back in his seat. 'It's my family estate. It's right that it goes to you and eventually our child.' He stopped and drew in a breath that made his chest rise. 'The money is in addition to the regular income I'll set up for you and the child. It will cover the running of the estate if necessary, though if managed well it will pay for itself and more. The current manager is excellent, and the new wine-maker too.'

Molly frowned. She knew the place had been in his family for generations—centuries, in fact. Yet he wanted to give it to her?

'You could sign it over to your son or daughter direct.'

Something stirred in his expression, but she didn't know what. 'No, Molly. I want you to have it. You love the place and it's…fitting.'

'I don't understand.'

Pietro looked back steadily. 'Call it reparation. I'd planned to marry you, so you'd have had a right to it anyway. Now you and our child can live there without feeling beholden to me. I know you wouldn't consider that.' His voice dropped to a bass rumble. 'You'll be totally independent.'

'What do you want in return?'

'Nothing.' He frowned. 'I understand it's hard for you to take my word.'

'Of course it is. You lied to me.' The anguish was still fresh.

'I didn't lie about caring for you. *I love you, Molly.*'

For the first time since Pietro had turned up on her doorstep she saw that familiar bright blaze of gold in his eyes. His words, and his searing look, shook her to the core. How badly she wanted to believe him. Even knowing it was a tactic to win her over, Molly felt its power, like an earth tremor cracking the foundations of her determination.

'You *would* say that.'

Pietro paled, those grooves near his mouth carving deeper as his lips twisted. To Molly's surprise he nodded. 'I knew I wouldn't be able to convince you. Yet I told myself…' He stopped and looked away. Then he sighed. 'The truth, the absolute truth, is that I love you, Molly. I can't tell you how sorry I am that I hurt you. That you felt betrayed.'

He swung back to fix her with a look that stole her breath. Pietro looked…haunted.

'It's true I lied because I wanted you and wanted my child. But the joke is on me, because I never recognised till too late that I was motivated the whole time by love. I fell in love with you in Tuscany. That's why I overreacted when you told me you were pregnant.'

'You have a strange way of showing your love.' Molly crossed her arms and set her chin high. She wouldn't fall for such a glib line.

'You're right. It was inexcusable. I'd had such a hellish experience with Elizabetta, I let it taint what we had. Looking back, it's hard to believe that I wondered, even for a moment, if you were made in the same mould as her—feigning pregnancy to get her hands on my money. My reaction was shameful, over the top. Nothing can excuse it.' He shot to his feet, hands thrust in his pockets as he paced.

This was more like the man she remembered. Vital, powerful, driven. Yet, when he turned to face her, it wasn't determination she read on his features. It looked like defeat.

'But it doesn't matter how much I explain or excuse myself. I lied to you. Which means you've got no reason to believe me now when I say I love you and want you for yourself, not because of the baby. There's nothing I can say or do to prove my feelings, is there?'

He looked down at her, his scrutiny so intent Molly's blood heated.

'You're right. Words are easy. It's deeds that count.'

A muscle flicked in Pietro's jaw and his nostrils flared on a swiftly indrawn breath.

He nodded, the movement an abrupt jerk of his neck.

'Then there's nothing more to be said.' He paused so long the silence pounded between them, heavy and full of pain. 'But if you need anything, at any time, don't hesitate to contact me.' He swallowed, the movement pronounced. 'Or if you prefer you can contact my lawyer.' He nodded to the papers. 'The details are there.'

Abruptly, so quickly Molly was caught by surprise, he turned to the door.

'That's it? Don't you want to hear when the baby is born, or get updates later?'

Pietro looked at her over his shoulder, his mouth lifting at one side. 'I know you, Molly. You'll do the decent thing and share that information with me, even if it's through an intermediary.'

For a moment longer he looked down at her, and it struck Molly that she'd never seen anything like the bleakness in Pietro's eyes. The lack of hope. The pain. Real pain. There was no mistaking it for anything else.

Then, before she could gather her thoughts, Pietro turned and left the room.

Molly was so stunned, it took a moment to realise he was heading down the hall to the front door. She listened to his footsteps with mounting disbelief.

Her ears buzzed. Her vision blurred. She stared dumbly at the document on her lap.

He'd come all this way to give her the deeds to his estate and now he was going? It seemed impossible even as it happened.

Why come so far to hand her a paper a solicitor could have passed on?

But he'd done more, hadn't he?

He'd apologised. He'd told her he loved her.

Molly's eyes shut, her heart thudding high against her breastbone as she recalled the pain in his eyes. No, more than pain. Despair.

Pietro wasn't that good an actor. Was he?

Tears of frustration and hurt burnt the back of her eyes as she fought the desire to believe him. How could she, without proof?

But there could never be independent proof of Pietro's love. No empirical evidence. Only his word and his actions. It was a question of trust.

Deeds speak louder than words.

That was what she'd said, wasn't it?

The blurred type before her gradually cleared and Molly's heart jumped as key phrases burned onto her retinas.

What had Pietro done?

He'd looked after her while she'd recuperated. He'd been considerate and protective. He'd devoted himself to her, at times neglecting his business to do so. He'd taken her to Tuscany, even though he must have wondered if the place would revive her memories.

He'd organised her flight home to Australia in first-class luxury, without argument and without being asked.

He'd located Jillian and brought her home too, without once seeking thanks.

He'd signed over the estate she knew was the place he'd been happiest, with his family.

And what had he asked for? Nothing. There'd been no coercion. Just the expectation that she'd do the right thing by updating him about their baby.

How loudly did those deeds speak?

Molly looked at the doorway through which he'd disappeared and the tears she'd held at bay flooded her eyes.

Love was a risk, no matter what the circumstances. Was it a risk she dared to take? She had her child to think of. Whatever decision she made would affect it too.

Could she make a leap of faith or should she play safe?

Pietro reached for the ignition but his hand shook so much he planted it instead on the steering wheel.

It wasn't just his hands. His body quaked as great, wracking tremors of anguish ripped through him. From seeing his beloved Molly, feeling that inevitable uprush of emotion, and being spurned again.

He told himself it would get better with time. He couldn't believe it, but daily all around the world people survived calamity on a massive scale. Surely he could survive this?

His mouth cracked open in a bitter laugh that tore at his lungs. He'd thought he'd suffered through his marriage to Elizabetta, but disappointment and hurt pride were insignificant specks of sand compared to the anguish tormenting him now.

It had taken all his willpower to respect Molly's wishes. Not to badger her to change her mind but turn away and leave.

He'd promised himself he wouldn't plead for forgiveness. Not because he was too proud, but because it would do no good. He'd seen the distrust shimmer in her fine eyes. Besides, if she'd given him another chance simply because she felt sorry for him, that wasn't enough.

Pietro wanted her *love*. He *needed* it.

Like he needed his next breath.

Grimly he stared at his white-knuckled hands. He *would* conquer this urge to stride back, sweep her off her feet and into his arms. To kiss her into surrender.

Surely he would.

Yet he couldn't banish the temptation to march in and *demand* she love him.

He was so intent on his thoughts the tap on the driver's window shocked him. But not as much as the thrill of disbelief as he met Molly's serious gaze through the glass.

Everything inside Pietro stilled as hope pulsed. He breathed deep, dragging oxygen into starved lungs. There was no reason to hope. Molly looked shell-shocked, not happy.

Slowly, bones aching like an old man's, he opened the door and got out. Molly moved back a step, but no further, and despite everything Pietro couldn't stop the spike of adrenalin in his blood.

She licked her lips. Inevitably heat coiled in his belly.

She looked at her hands, her brow knotting, and Pietro's heart dived.

Then she raised her face and the glow he saw there made his pulse hike.

'I believe you.'

'Sorry?' He saw her lips move but her voice was so soft he found himself leaning in, inhaling her fresh, sweet scent.

'I believe you.' Stronger this time, more definite. 'I trust you, Pietro.' She broke into a tremulous smile that did the most remarkable things to his vital organs.

For a suspended moment speech was impossible, or movement. Then Pietro did what he'd been fighting not to do since he arrived. He pulled Molly to him, wrapping one arm tightly around her so they fit together. He lifted his other hand to her face. Her chin was already angled up as she surveyed him with that wide, wondrous, heart-stopping smile. He settled his hand on her cheek and a dart of pure love pierced him as she turned her face into his touch.

'You do?' His voice was a stranger's, drawn and rough.

'I do.' Her hand palmed his cheek and it felt like heaven. His pulse thundered.

'You forgive me?'

Molly nodded, her smile becoming a grin that rivalled the sun for brilliance.

'I love you, Pietro. I fell in love with you a long time ago. I want to spend the rest of my life with you.'

He rocked back on his heels, overcome. His voice, when he finally found it, was dredged straight from his heart. 'I love you too, Molly. I fell in love with you a long time ago. I want to spend the rest of my life with you. And I promise to live up to your trust.'

Molly sighed. 'I couldn't ask for more.'

Pietro leaned down and took her mouth with his. It was a tender kiss, a testament to the wellspring of love they shared.

Ages later, when the kiss had grown hot and hungry, and Molly had plastered herself all over him as if she couldn't get enough, the toot of a car horn made Pietro look up. Several of Molly's neighbours were on the street, ostensibly going to cars or checking letter boxes, all sending curious glances their way.

'We're shocking the neighbours,' she murmured.

'Do you mind?' He didn't give a damn what anyone thought, so long as he had Molly.

'Not at all.' She smiled and that slam of emotion hit him anew—desire and excitement and love. 'I want to share my news with everyone.'

'Then you won't mind this.' He swung her high into his arms and strode across the road to the little green house.

Molly's laughter rang in his ears all the way across the street, into her house and down the hall to her bedroom.

It was a sound Pietro knew he'd never tire of. She was his woman. His future. His love.

EPILOGUE

'Signora Agosti?'

'Si?' Molly turned to see Marta in the bedroom doorway, glamorous in a dark-crimson dress. She was off duty today, staying at the Tuscan villa with the other guests.

'The photographer is ready, *signora*. Do you need help?'

'No need, thanks, Marta. I'm here now.' It was Pietro who spoke, appearing in the doorway behind the housekeeper. His eyes met Molly's and she felt that squiggle of heat through her insides as his mouth tipped at the corner in the smile reserved just for her. Then he turned to the older woman. 'Tell them we'll be along straight away.'

Yet Marta paused beside him. 'Just remember, *signore*, that your wife won't want to look rumpled in the photos.'

Pietro huffed out a laugh as he strode across the bedroom, stopping only when he could reach out and take his wife's hand. 'Marta knows me too well.'

Molly saw the devilry in his eyes and shook her head. 'Don't even think about it. I just touched up my lipstick! For once I want to look presentable in a photo, not—'

'Rumpled?' His deep voice wound through her like a velvet chord, stroking her senses awake.

'Exactly.' She looked up into those hooded, golden eyes and had to repress a laugh as his mouth twisted in obvious disappointment.

'But, *tesoro*. One little kiss.' His other hand slid around her waist, drawing her close.

Molly's blood beat hard and fast, flushing her cheeks, reminding her how very hard it was to resist Pietro.

Before she could stop him he leaned closer, pressing his lips to the corner of her mouth, then trailing heated kisses down her throat, making her sigh and arch back against his arm. Heat speared to her middle, arrowing in on that needy place between her legs.

'Pietro!' She was shocked when he lifted his head to grin down at her. His laughing eyes told her he knew how cheated she felt, despite her earlier admonition.

'Don't fret.' Again that intimate smile that made her heart dance. 'As soon as the photos are over, I promise to bring you back upstairs to…rest.' He waggled his eyebrows suggestively.

'And who'll look after our guests?'

'Chiara and Jillian have already offered. They thought you'd be tired after the christening party.' His warm breath feathered her ear, making her shiver. 'They have no idea how…robust you are. Delightfully so.'

His hand tracked down from her waist with definite intent. But, despite her instant rise of anticipation, Molly caught his marauding hand and pulled it away.

'Later, Pietro. The photos, remember? We girls want to look beautiful for posterity.'

He turned her hand, linking her fingers with his. 'You're always beautiful, *mio dolce amore*, inside and out. And as for the girls…' He turned to where the twins slumbered side by side in their cots, looking adorable with their dark curls and rosebud mouths. 'They're almost as beautiful as their mother.'

Molly disagreed. In her eyes Margherita and Marcella were the most gorgeous people in the world. Even their names held a special place in her heart. Pietro had demanded that one be named for her and her grandmother, following her family's tradition. And Molly had decided on Marcella, in memory of Pietro's little sister.

'Thank you, my darling.' Pietro raised her hand to his lips. 'I never believed I could be so happy.'

Her heart sang as she smiled up at him. 'Neither did I.' Then she leaned in and, forgetting all about the photos, kissed him full on the lips.

Her man. Her love.

* * * * *

If you enjoyed
Her Forgotten Lover's Heir,
*you're sure to enjoy these other stories
by Annie West!*

The Desert King's Captive Bride
His Majesty's Temporary Bride
The Greek's Forbidden Princess
Contracted for the Petrakis Heir
Inherited for the Royal Bed

Available now!

#3677 AN INNOCENT, A SEDUCTION, A SECRET
One Night With Consequences
by Abby Green
When Seb spies Edie's talent for lavish interior decoration, he makes an irresistible job offer—spend the festive season decorating his opulent home! But soon, Edie becomes the sensual gift Seb wishes to unwrap...

#3678 THE BILLIONAIRE'S CHRISTMAS CINDERELLA
by Carol Marinelli
Abe Devereux is famed for his cold heart. So meeting Naomi, who's determined to see the good in him, is a novelty. But will seducing her be his biggest risk, or his greatest chance of redemption?

#3679 PREGNANT BY THE DESERT KING
by Susan Stephens
Lucy is shocked by Tadj's royal revelation: Lucy is carrying the baby of a desert king! Tadj will secure his heir, but can Lucy accept his scandalous solution—that she share his royal bed?

#3680 THE VIRGIN'S SICILIAN PROTECTOR
by Chantelle Shaw
Hired to keep heiress Ariana safe, wealthy bodyguard Santino is intrigued by her hidden vulnerability. Their sexual tension is electric! And when Santino discovers just how innocent Ariana is, resisting her temptation becomes an impossible challenge...

Get 4 FREE REWARDS!

We'll send you 2 FREE Books plus 2 FREE Mystery Gifts.

FREE
Value Over
$20

Harlequin Presents® books feature a sensational and sophisticated world of international romance where sinfully tempting heroes ignite passion.

SPECIAL EXCERPT FROM

⊕ HARLEQUIN

Presents.

Santo's stunned to see Giovanna again. Why, after
that one forbidden night, did she leave? But when Gia
reveals their secret consequence, the Italian will claim
his son—and Gia as his wife!

Read on for a sneak preview of
Jennifer Hayward's next story,
Married for a One-Night Consequence.

He set his glass down with a clatter. "I am his *father*. I
have missed three years of his life. You think a *weekend
pass* is going to suffice? A few dips in the Caribbean as he
learns to swim?" He fixed his gaze on hers. "I want *every
day* with him. I want it *all*."

"What else can we do?" she queried helplessly. "You
live in New York and I live here. Leo is settled and
happy. A limited custody arrangement is the only realistic
proposition."

"It is *not* a viable proposition." His low growl made
her jump. "That's not going to work, Gia."

She eyed him warily. "Which part?"

"All of it." He waved a Rolex-clad wrist at her. "I
have a proposal for you. It's the only one on the table,
nonnegotiable on all points. Take it or leave it."

The wariness written across her face intensified. "Which is?"

"We do what's in the best interests of our child. You marry me, we create a life together in New York and give Leo the family he deserves."

Don't miss
Married for a One-Night Consequence,
available December 2018 wherever
Harlequin Presents® books and ebooks are sold.

www.Harlequin.com

HARLEQUIN

Presents®

Coming next month—a festive trio just in time
for the holidays!

Claiming His Christmas Wife by Dani Collins

Part of the Conveniently Wed! miniseries

When Imogen faints in the cold New York snow,
Travis is called to his ex-wife's very public rescue!
But, with a deal *just* for Christmas, will he be able
to let Imogen go a second time?

Bound by Their Christmas Baby by Clare Connelly

Part of the Christmas Seductions miniseries

When brooding bachelor Gabe learns Abby is his business
rival's daughter, he's furious. So what will he do when she
returns the following Christmas with their secret baby?

The Billionaire's Christmas Cinderella by Carol Marinelli

Tycoon Abe is overwhelmed by the potency of his
undeniable connection with Naomi. Now he wants
this shy Cinderella between his sheets by Christmas!

Available December 2018

HPBPA1118